The Billionaire's Club

Meet the world's most eligible bachelors...
by
Rebecca Winters

For tycoons Vincenzo Gagliardi,
Takis Manolis and Cesare Donati,
transforming the Castello di Lombardi into
one of Europe's most highly sought-after hotels
will be more than just a business venture—
it's a challenge to be relished!

But these three men,
bound by a friendship as strong as blood,
are about to discover that the chase is only half
the fun as three women conquer their hearts
and change their lives for ever...

Return of Her Italian Duke
Bound to Her Greek Billionaire
Whisked Away by Her Sicilian Boss

Available now!

Dear Reader,

Whisked Away by Her Sicilian Boss is the third book in The Billionaire's Club miniseries.

The devilishly handsome Cesare Donati is the last of the three friends and business partners who own the Castello Supremo Hotel and Ristorante di Lombardi in Milan to meet the woman who was made for him.

Before she comes into his life he can't really see himself ever settling down to marriage. Then suddenly, while he's conducting the business that has made him so successful, out of nowhere there she is! The gorgeous Tuccia Leonardi, who has fled from a fate worse than death, runs straight into Cesare's arms.

An accident, or destiny? I'll let you, the reader, decide.

Enjoy!

Rebecca Winters

WHISKED AWAY
BY HER
SICILIAN BOSS

BY
REBECCA WINTERS

First Published in Great Britain 2017
By Mills & Boon, an imprint of HarperCollins*Publishers*
1 London Bridge Street, London, SE1 9GF

© 2017 Rebecca Winters

ISBN: 978-0-263-06991-4

Our policy is to use papers that are natural, renewable and recyclable
products and made from wood grown in sustainable forests. The logging
and manufacturing processes conform to the legal environmental
regulations of the country of origin.

Printed and bound in Great Britain
by CPI Antony Rowe, Chippenham, Wiltshire

Rebecca Winters lives in Salt Lake City, Utah. With canyons and high alpine meadows full of wildflowers, she never runs out of places to explore. They, plus her favourite vacation spots in Europe, often end up as backgrounds for her romance novels—because writing is her passion, along with her family and church. Rebecca loves to hear from readers. If you wish to email her, please visit her website at cleanromances.com.

To all of you readers who have read my books
and let me know you enjoy them.

You'll never know what your kind, encouraging
words do to make this author's job a pure delight!

Thank you from the bottom of my heart.

CHAPTER ONE

Salon des Reines, Paris, France

THE CHAUFFEUR OF Le Comte Jean-Michel Ardois pulled the limousine up in front of the bridal salon on the Rue de L'Echelle. In the last two weeks Princess Tuccianna Falcone Leonardi of Sicily had been here with her mother three times for the bridal dress fitting. Each time they'd come, she'd made excuses to visit the bathroom in order to study the layout of the exclusive shop.

This morning was her final fitting to make sure everything was perfect for the wedding ceremony tomorrow. Only Tuccia had no intention of showing up for the elaborate nuptials arranged by her parents and Comte Ardois ten years ago in a horrifying, iron-clad betrothal forced upon her. She'd dreamed of her freedom forever. Now had come the moment for her escape.

Madame Dufy, the owner, welcomed them inside. After fussing over Tuccia and telling her how excited she was for her forthcoming marriage to the *comte*, she took them back to the dressing room befitting a queen.

"Delphine will be with you in just a moment with your gown. It's as exquisite as you are, Princess."

The second she left, Tuccia turned to her mother, the Marchesa di Trabia of Sicily. "I need to go to the restroom."

"Surely not!"

"I can't help it. You know how I get when I'm nervous."

"You are impossible, Tuccia!"

"If I don't go, it might happen in here."

Her mother's hands flew up in the air. "All right! But don't take too long. We have a long list of things that must be done today."

"I'll hurry, Mamma."

Yes, she'd hurry. Right out of the clutches of the *comte*!

She knew he planned to assign her a bodyguard the moment they were married and never let her out of his sight for the rest of their lives. After overhearing him discuss it with her parents, who'd said she needed a strong hand, she'd been planning how to disappear.

Tuccia opened the door and walked down the hall to the door of the bathroom. But she only went inside to leave her betrothal ring on the floor near the sink. Whoever found it could think what they wanted. After looking around to make sure no one had seen her, she rushed down another hallway straight out the back door of the shop.

From there it was only a short run down the alley used for delivery trucks to the street where she climbed in a taxi.

"Le Bourget Aeroport, *s'il vous plait.*"

Her heart refused to stop thudding as they drove

off. She looked behind her. No one had come running out of the alley chasing after her yet. Tuccia prayed all the way to the airport where she boarded an Eljet chartered for her under a fake name and paid for her by her aunt Bertina. Once it landed in Palermo, Sicily, she'd take a taxi to her aunt's palazzo.

Before long Tuccia's favorite person in the whole world would be offering her sanctuary. Her life would continue to depend on Bertina's help, or all was lost.

The next day, Milan, Italy

Dinner had concluded in the private dining room of the legendary fourteenth-century *castello*, the home of the former first Duc di Lombardi in Milan, Italy.

Vincenzo Gagliardi, the present-day *duc*, lifted his goblet with the insignia of the Gagliardi coat of arms. "*Buona fortuna* this trip, Cesare. Our business is depending on you. May you return with my wife's replacement soon. The baby will be here in two months. I want Gemma off her feet ASAP."

"Amen," Takis declared, raising his glass. "You're going to have to be quick, *amico*." He touched his goblet to Cesare's, and they sipped the local vintage Lombardia that Vincenzo had produced from the vast wine cellar for his send-off.

Cesare Donati eyed his two best friends with a smile. They'd been like brothers to him for more than a decade. Together they'd turned the former fortress palace of Vincenzo's family into the five-star Castello Supremo Hotel and Ristorante di Lombardi, Europe's most sought-after resort.

"I have a surprise for you. I'll be back in two days

with our new pastry chef. I told Gemma as much this morning."

"That soon?" they said in unison.

"It's been arranged for a while, so have no concerns."

His friends smiled in relief. For Cesare's contribution to their successful enterprise, he'd already found the perfect person to replace Gemma as the *castello*'s new executive pastry chef.

But he'd been keeping the identity of his choice a secret until he could present Ciro Fragala in person with one of his many specialties for their delectation.

Vincenzo's wife had learned to make Florentine pastry from her mother who'd cooked for the last *duc*. Though her cooking was perfection and drew the elite clientele that came to the *castello*, in Cesare's opinion the best cook in the world was his own Sicilian mother.

She'd learned from the nuns who made divine pastries and ran the orphanage where she'd been raised until she turned eighteen. On her say-so—and she would know better than anyone else—Cesare had done the necessary research on Signor Fragala, the pastry cook she'd declared to be the finest in all Sicily. After a visit to the Palermo restaurant with his mother two months ago, he'd agreed totally with her assessment.

Hiring Ciro meant sensational new desserts for their business enterprise in Milan. The two of them had met with the fifty-five-year-old widower several times in the last few weeks. The chef had said he would leap at the chance to work at the famous *castello* restaurant.

Since he didn't have children, it wouldn't be a problem to move. He'd given his notice and Cesare planned to fly him to Milan. The new chef would work well with their executive French chef at the *castello*. Most of all, the guys would be pleased by the man's amiable personality.

"We'll drive you to the airport," Vincenzo stated.

Cesare shook his head. "Thanks, but you've done enough by surprising me with this dinner. You've both got pregnant wives who've been generous enough to let us have this meal together. By now they'll be wondering where you are. The limo is waiting as we speak."

"Then we'll walk you out," Vincenzo murmured.

"Grazie."

He drained the rest of his wine and got to his feet. Reaching for the suitcase he'd left by the double doors, he moved ahead of them to the portrait-lined corridor of the former *ducs* with their legendary silvery eyes.

"Stay safe," Takis said as Cesare climbed in the rear of the limo.

"Always."

Vincenzo smiled. "We can't wait to meet this mystery paragon of pastry chefs." He patted Cesare's shoulder and shut the door before it drove away from the *castello*.

Two hours later, the Lombardi ducal jet arrived at Palermo International Airport, where another limousine waited for him on the tarmac. Cesare told the driver to take him to the posh Mondello borough. It was there he'd bought a villa in the famed *art nouveau* style for his mother and sister who was now married and lived in the city with her husband and their toddler.

He'd wanted nothing but the best for his wonderful mamma, Lina Donati.

She would never leave Palermo. After being raised by the nuns and learning how to cook from them, she'd started out working in a local restaurant after leaving the orphanage.

Her subsequent marriage was short-lived. Abandoned by her husband, she'd cooked her way through life to support their little family and had made a name for herself. Cesare believed she made the best food on earth. In her honor he'd had a state-of-the-art kitchen installed because he couldn't do enough for her.

Thanks to a bad back from being on her feet all the time, she now cooked exclusively for Bertina Spadaro, who wasn't a demanding employer. Cesare had begged her to retire. He would take care of her forever. But his mother said she couldn't imagine not having work to do and she loved Bertina. The aristocratic older sister of the Marchesa di Leonardi di Trabia had become her friend.

The Leonardi family descended from the royal Sicilian family of the commune of Trabia, thirty miles from Palermo, and could trace their roots back to the 1400s, when the land and castle were granted them by Frederick III. The present *marchese* and *marchesa* had established their own *palazzo* in the heart of Palermo.

Bertina and Lina had become fast friends over the years and were in each other's confidence. The rest of the time his mother spent with Cesare's family, or tended her spectacular herb garden.

The elite area of Mondello had everything: exclusive yachting clubs dotting its sandy beach, restaurants, shops and a marina with numerous yachts, including the *marchese*'s gleaming white royal yacht that stood out from the others.

Before buying the villa for her, Cesare, too, had been captivated as he'd walked through the sand of its private beach front, inhaling the air filled with the heady scent of orange blossoms and jasmine. Whenever he flew to Palermo, Cesare was reminded that with all its rich history, there was nowhere else in the world he found more fascinating.

But tonight as they drove into the ancient, colorful city, he was met with the strong smells of fish and spices that always brought back memories of his youth. There was a hint of the old Arab souks, taking him back to his childhood. As a boy, these streets with their subtle niches and labyrinths had been his backyard.

His father had been in the merchant marines, but ran off before Cesare was a year old, leaving his mother to work in a trattoria and support him and his older sister Isabella. They'd lived in the apartment above it in a rougher neighborhood of Palermo. Cesare's world had been filled with lots of purse snatchers, few showers that usually didn't work, grueling heat. Everything had been run-down and chaotic.

Since he'd been too young to remember his father, he didn't miss him, only the idea of him. Cesare had envied his friends who had fathers and taught them things. Early in life he'd felt embarrassed at times that he was the only one who went to mass unaccompanied while the other boys walked in the church with their own fathers.

As he grew up, the embarrassment went away, but he lacked the confidence he saw in his friends whose sense of belonging seemed to give them an extra layer of it.

Cesare couldn't comprehend a man abandoning his wife and children, never caring about them again. Sometimes in his teens he'd dreamed about meeting his father, but those dreams were unsatisfactory because his father always turned away from him. The dreams eventually stopped, but not the feeling that there was something lacking in him.

At the age of thirty, Cesare was living a different life. Thanks to the college mentor who'd taught him and his partners how to invest, his worth now figured in the billions. But the past could never be forgotten and had formed him into the man he'd become.

Over time he'd seen enough to decide romantic love was transitory at most. Of course there were exceptions, like his partners' marriages. But at this stage in his life Cesare wasn't that confident that he was marriage material. He hadn't witnessed two parents loving each other. So far he felt he was better off alone like his mother. With a sister and brother-in-law and their daughter Elana, Cesare was happy enough with the family he loved.

In fact he had all he needed, including the occasional relationship with a woman. There was no guarantee that one would stay with him if he did get married, or that it would last.

Or that he might not be more like his father than he thought...

From time to time that thought haunted him because he hadn't met a woman who meant everything to him. Maybe he'd subconsciously pushed them away so he didn't have to deal with commitment. Though he didn't want to bring up past pain to his mother, one of these days he would have a talk with her about the man who'd disappeared on their family, on *him*.

When the limo finally reached the villa, Cesare put his darker thoughts away and paid the driver before getting out. His mother was expecting him, and knew he'd be flying Ciro Fragala back to Milan with him the next day. But it was close to one o'clock. She always went to bed early.

He'd told her not to wait up and they'd talk in the morning before Ciro arrived at the villa in a limo Cesare had arranged for ahead of time. The man would be shipping his belongings to Milan and he'd stay in a room at the *castello* until he decided where he wanted to live.

Every time Cesare came to Palermo, he was charmed by the large ochre-colored villa spread over two floors with three beautiful terraces and a Mediterranean garden. The small pool was lined with glazed tiles of North African origin.

From the terrace off the dining room he was met with a glorious view of the Gulf front. It was a sight he'd always loved after climbing the bluff called Mount Pellegrino many times in his youth. From there he could imagine himself escaping the suffocating heat and madness of the city and sailing away to America. Incredibly that dream had come true.

Once he'd entered the foyer, he turned off the outside light and moved across the stone tiles of the villa in the dark to the kitchen with his suitcase. After setting it down, his first instinct was to grab himself a small bottle of his favorite *grappa digestivo* from the cabinet where he knew it was kept, then head upstairs to his suite with it. Before sleep, all he wanted was to take a few sips to remind him he was back in the land of his roots.

But as he turned to pick up his suitcase, he bumped into another body and heard a cry.

"Mamma?" He automatically hugged her to him. "*Mi dispiace tanto.* I didn't think you'd be up this late. Did I hurt you?"

That's when the bottle slipped from his hand and cracked on the floor. But the strong scent of the 60 proof alcohol wasn't nearly as shocking as the feel of the woman in his arms.

She wasn't built anything like his wiry brunette mother or her housekeeper who came in several times a week. In fact she was taller than both of them. To add to his surprise, the flowery scent from her hair and skin intoxicated him. It took him a second to gather his wits.

"Don't move. There's broken glass. I'll turn on the light." He let her go and walked to the doorway to flip the switch. Cesare was shocked yet again.

If he didn't know better, he would think he'd released a gorgeous enchanted princess from her bottle. Her stunning figure was swathed in a lemon silk robe. Thank heaven she was wearing sandals. Between her medium-length black curls and eyes gray as the morning mist off the ocean, his gaze managed to swallow her whole before he realized she looked familiar to him. He knew he'd seen her before but couldn't place her.

She stared back as if disbelieving before taking a few steps away from the wet mess on the stone flooring. A hand went to her throat. "You're Cesare," she murmured, sounding astonished.

"I'm afraid you've got me at a disadvantage, *signorina*." Maybe he was in the middle of a fantastic dream, but so far he hadn't awakened. Quickly he walked over to the utility closet for a cloth and brush to pick up the glass and clean the floor.

"My name is Tuccia. I'm so sorry to have startled you."

Tuccia. An unusual name.

Tuccia. Short for... Princess Tuccianna of Sicilian nobililty?

Over the years there'd been photos of her in the newspapers from time to time, mostly stories about her escapades away from the royal *palazzo* where she got into trouble with friends and was seen partying in local clubs to the embarrassment of the royal household. But Cesare had never seen her up close.

The latest news in the Palermo press reported she was engaged to be married to some French *comte* who lived in Paris and was one of the wealthiest men in France.

No. It couldn't be, yet he realized it *was* she.

"I'm afraid I don't recognize it," he dissembled until he could work out why the daughter of the Marchese and Marchesa of the ancient Sicilian House of Trabia, was in his mother's villa.

"You probably wouldn't. It's not common."

She was trying to put Cesare off, but he intended to get to the bottom of this mystery. "Did Mamma hire you to be a new maid?"

She averted her eyes. "No. Signora Donati allowed me to stay with her for tonight." He frowned, not having known anything about this. Why hadn't his beloved mother told him what to expect when he arrived? "I—I thought I heard a noise, *signor,*" she stammered, "but I didn't have time to turn on the light."

"No. We were both taken by surprise," he murmured, still reeling from the sensation of her incredible body clutched to his so she wouldn't fall.

Cesare had enjoyed various relationships with attractive women over the years, but he'd never gotten into anything serious. Yet the feel and sight of the beautiful young princess, whose face was like something out of Botticelli, had shaken him.

"I guess you know you have the most wonderful mother in the world," she gushed all of a sudden, breaking in on his private thoughts. He was amazed by her comment. It had sounded completely sincere.

He closed the utility door and turned to her, growing more curious by the second. "I do. How did you two meet?"

His question caused her to hesitate. "I think it would be better if you ask her. I'm truly sorry to have disturbed you and will say goodnight." She darted away, leaving him full of questions and standing there wide awake in the trail of her fragrance.

The princess, reputed to be a spoiled, headstrong handful, had elegance and manners. *Damn* if she didn't also have an unaffected charm that had worked its way beneath his skin.

He took a deep breath. Though Cesare didn't like waking his mother, he knew there'd be no sleep until

he had answers. Before heading upstairs to her bedroom, he opened the cabinet for another bottle of
grappa. All he found was a half-opened bottle of
cooking sherry.

That's what he got for not turning on the light earlier. That and the memory of a moment in time he
feared wasn't about to let him go.

With a pounding out-of-control heart, twenty-five-
year-old Principessa Tuccianna Falcone Leonardi
rushed to the guest room down the hall at the rear
of the villa. She should never have made a trip to the
kitchen, but needed something to drink. Lina had told
her to help herself to anything, including the soda she
kept on hand in the fridge.

Being crushed unexpectedly against a hard male
body in the dark had come as such a huge surprise that
her mind and body were still reeling. She could still
feel the male power of him and smell the faint scent
of the soap he'd used in the shower. The combination
had completely disarmed her.

After he'd turned on the kitchen light, she'd had her
first look at Lina's tall, incredibly attractive brown-
haired son. Tuccia knew of him, but had no idea that
Lina had given birth to the most striking man she'd
ever seen in her life. Those deep blue eyes and his
masculine potency had managed to make such an in-
delible impression her heart still kept turning over
on itself.

"I didn't know there was a man in Palermo who
looked like that," she whispered to herself. Tuccia was
positive there wasn't another one in all Europe who
could match him.

More than ever she was revolted at the thought of marrying her forty-year-old French fiancé who had only stared at her with lust. The fabulously wealthy Comte Jean-Michel Ardois, who would soon inherit the title after his ailing father passed away, was always trying to touch her, and lately more and more inappropriately.

On occasion she'd seen him be quite ruthless with the people who worked for the Ardois family. He was a cold, calculating man whom she could never love or bring herself to marry.

Her betrothal at the age of sixteen had been a political necessity arranged by her parents, the Marchese and Marchesa di Trabia, whose funds needed constant bolstering. Since that time she'd felt doomed to an existence she'd dreaded with every fiber of her being.

After careful planning, she'd seized the moment to run away twenty-four hours before the ceremony was to take place. Taking flight from the boutique, she'd flown back to her home in Sicily. Thanks to her Zia Bertina, her mother's widowed elder sister, she'd been given the help she needed to escape on that jet.

Bertina lived in her own palazzo in Palermo where she entertained close friends and loved Tuccia like the child she'd never been able to have. Tuccia's *zia* was a romantic who'd always been in sympathy with her niece's tragic situation, and had prevailed on her cook, Lina Donati, to let her hide at her villa overnight. In the meantime she was still trying to arrange transport for Tuccia to stay with a distant cousin living in Podgorica in Montenegro until the worst of the scandal had passed.

But Tuccia had placed her in a terrible position.

Bertina had continued living in the palazzo after her husband died, but she needed monetary help on occasion. Tuccia's *zio*, Pietro Spadaro, hadn't been a wealthy man. If Tuccia's parents got angry enough at Bertina, they could stop giving her extra money. They might throw her out of the only home she'd known since her marriage.

Worse, if they knew Bertina had involved a cousin in another country, let alone asked such a desperate favor of her adored cook to help solve Tuccia's problems, who knew how ugly the situation could get. If Bertina were forced to lose the palazzo and any extra money, she wouldn't be able to pay Lina for being her cook. Lina could be out of a job for harboring her. All of it would be her fault.

She couldn't believe her bad luck in running into Lina's son. Naturally he was going to wonder why she was here and question his mother. What she needed to do was get dressed and pack her bag so she'd be ready to steal from the villa at dawn before anyone was up.

Tuccia knew a full-scale search by Jean-Michel and her parents had been underway for her since she had disappeared from the salon. At least with her gone from Lina's villa, Bertina wouldn't be implicated.

She had saved enough money to take a bus and travel to Catania where she could get a job through a friend who would help her. If she were careful, she could subsist for a while. She didn't dare access her bank account even though its pitiful balance had never been big enough to pay for as much as an airline ticket.

Tuccia had no idea how long she would have to remain hidden. But even if it meant being disowned and disinherited, it didn't matter because she'd rather be dead than have to marry Jean-Michel. She was sickened at the thought of him taking her to bed, let alone living with him for a lifetime.

CHAPTER TWO

CESARE SAT AT the side of his mother's bed, still trying to comprehend what she'd just told him. "Apparently you and Princess Tuccianna have enjoyed a relationship you never told me about."

"Only since I started cooking for Bertina two years ago. Until tonight I'd been sworn to secrecy. She needs help desperately, Cesare."

He reached for her hand. "Don't you know what a terrible position this has put you in, Mamma? The authorities from two governments are looking everywhere for her. Her jilted fiancé could be dangerous. He has the kind of money and power that could crush you. If her parents found out you gave her shelter, your name could be ruined. You could lose your job with Bertina. They could make life miserable for you."

"It's Tuccia's life I'm worried about, not mine. You know how I feel about titles. It's a feudal system. No young woman should have to marry a man almost twice her age because of money and power. You can't imagine how frightened Bertina is for her niece. The *comte* will impose his will on her. She's very beautiful. And you know exactly what I'm talking about."

Cesare was afraid he did. He'd seen first-hand the

trouble that kind of will had created for Vincenzo and Vincenzo's cousin Dimi. The two had grown up together at the *castello* and had suffered through tragedy together because of overpowering parental dominance over both of them.

After Cesare had become close friends with the two royals he had learned their story, so he understood why the princess refused to be tied legally to a man who could do what he wanted to his young, helpless wife. Cesare was sickened by it himself, but his protective instincts had kicked in for his mother. He didn't want her to be a part of this and he got up from the bed.

"How long have you agreed to let her stay with you?"

"Until Bertina has worked out an escape plan to get her to a distant relative in Montenegro no one will trace."

He shook his head. "Of course they will! That's no plan," he bit out.

"I agree with you and I don't like any of it, either. But the princess is desperate. Bertina has told me that the father, Comte Ardois, was promiscuous and notoriously unfaithful over the years. She has it on good authority that his son Comte Jean-Michel is exactly the same way.

"He's had a mistress on the side for a long time. I can't bear that kind of life for her. Neither can she! Tuccia is like a lamb going to the slaughter. To me it's criminal!"

"What you're telling me sounds like a repeat of the stories Vincenzo told me about life at the *castello* growing up."

"So you do understand that Tuccia is a young sweet girl and needs to get far away from him while she still can."

"Yes, but not at your expense."

"Someone has to step up. If I lose my job because of this, I'll find another one. If that isn't possible, then I *will* let you take care of me. The point is, the *marchesa* and her husband have never been concerned about their daughter's feelings. They've spent their whole lives doing their royal duty and expect the same from Tuccia. The princess is alone in this. If Bertina hadn't chartered that jet for her so she could leave Paris, Tuccia would have been forced to walk down the aisle today and be married to a monster."

His hands went to his hips. "But now she has *you* involved."

"Because I want to be. I like Tuccia very much. If she were my daughter, I'd do whatever I could to save her from such a wretched life. You're the most brilliant, clever man I've ever known, *figlio mio*. If I asked for your help this one time, would you do it for your mamma?"

Her blue eyes beseeched him. She was serious! He could see it and feel it.

"What do you think I could do?"

"Fly her to Milan tomorrow on the Gagliardi ducal jet with Ciro. Help her find a place to stay in the city where no one will think to look for her. She won't be traced."

His eyes narrowed. "Is this the reason you let her stay here tonight? Because you knew I was flying in and planned to use me?"

"Yes," she answered with her usual refreshing hon-

esty. "Have I ever asked you for a favor like this before? Time is of the essence."

"Mamma—" His head reared in exasperation.

She sat up straighter in the bed. "I don't see a problem. Tuccia's crisis takes priority. That girl needs to
be far away from here by tomorrow. It won't hurt you
to take her with you. Be sure she's wearing a disguise.
Signor Fragala won't suspect who she is."

He stopped pacing. "He'll recognize her once we're
on board."

"So you'll swear him to secrecy. If he can't be
trusted, tell him you've changed your mind and won't
let him have the coveted chef position after all. It's
in *your* hands. Once you've settled her, you can take
Ciro to the *castello* and get on with your business. Is
that such a terrible thing to ask this one time?"

Cesare couldn't fathom that they were having this
conversation at three in the morning. "There's no
place she won't be recognized."

"Then take her to the *castello* with you. Smuggle
her in a back entrance and hide her in one of the turret rooms for a few days. That will give her enough
time to figure out a solid plan on her own. Besides
being well-educated and well-traveled, she's a very
intelligent girl and resourceful."

"And according to the papers, impossible," he added.

"If you knew the truth, you wouldn't judge her.
Every time her name gets in the news, it's because
she has tried to run away from her family. But she
always gets caught and is brought back. Her parents
cover it up by saying that she's an indulged, immature
troublemaker. She's the loveliest girl I've ever known,
and it's a tragedy how her life has been."

Such accolades for the princess shocked him. His mother wasn't about to relent on this. She was a fighter who had a heart of gold. That was how she'd made it through life.

"You'll help me to help her, won't you?"

Cesare loved and admired his mother more than any woman he'd ever known. After the hundreds of sacrifices she'd made for him and his sister growing up, how could he possibly turn her down?

Letting out a sigh he said, "Stop worrying. After Ciro arrives in the morning, I'll take her to Milan tomorrow with us." But not to the *castello.* He didn't want the guys to know what was going on.

"If you'll do that for me, I'll love you forever."

"I thought you already did," he teased.

Her eyes had filled with tears. "Oh, Cesare. My dear son. *Ti amo.*" She started to get out of bed, but her phone rang. Her eyes darted to his in alarm. "Maybe something's wrong with your sister or my little granddaughter—"

Cesare's body stiffened. A phone call in the middle of the night could mean anything. Probably it was Bertina calling his mother to tell her the police were on their way over to the villa looking for the princess.

She reached for the cell phone on her bedside table and checked the caller ID. "It says San Giovanni Hospital."

He stood stock-still while he waited to find out what was going on, but his mother did little talking. Once she hung up, she looked at him with haunted eyes.

"I'm afraid I have very bad news for you, Cesare."

"What do you mean?"

"Ciro was rushed to the hospital a few hours ago

with an infected lung and kidney. I thought he didn't seem well when I visited the restaurant a few days ago and assumed he had a cold.

"He must undergo an operation to drain off the fluid. The nurse said he had the presence of mind to ask the hospital to contact me before he lost consciousness."

"Santo Cielo," Cesare murmured in disbelief. This whole night had turned into a bad dream. "The poor devil."

"It's terrible."

"Get dressed and we'll drive to the hospital in your car. Since he's my responsibility, I'll tell the hospital and take care of his medical bills."

"Bless you. I'm getting ready now, but I'll visit him alone and be your go-between until he has recovered. Right now you've got to take care of the princess. The sooner, the better. That phone call could have been Bertina alerting me that the police were on Tuccia's trail. There's no time to lose."

There was no time for sleep, either, not while this situation continued. He walked to his suite to shower and change clothes for the flight back to Milan. Afterward he went downstairs to the kitchen to fix himself coffee. He found the delicious sweet rolls filled with ricotta and chocolate his mother always made for him when he came and ate several.

During his early morning feast, his mother joined him before leaving for the hospital. After she went out to her car, he contacted the pilot to let him know they'd be returning to Milan shortly, then he arranged for a limo to come to the villa. Now all he needed was for the princess to make an appearance.

* * *

It was six-thirty in the morning when Tuccia finished
writing three letters at the desk in the guest bedroom.
The first was her deepest apology to Jean-Michel,
explaining why she couldn't marry him and had run
away. They weren't in love with each other, and that
was the only reason for two people to marry.

She put it in an envelope with his name and address
on the front. When and where to mail it was the scary
part and had to be considered carefully because her
life depended on it.

Tuccia put the letter in her purse, then wrote two
long thank-you letters to her *zia* and Lina. She signed
them with love before leaving them on top of the
dresser so Lina would be certain to see them. One
of these days she would write to her parents, but that
could wait.

After making the bed, she grabbed the small suitcase Bertina had loaned her and hurried through the
villa to the kitchen for a piece of fruit. A ten-minute
walk would take her to the shops where she could eat
something more substantial and catch a bus.

"Where do you think you're going in that disguise?"
a deep familiar male voice asked as she reached the
foyer.

Her camouflage consisted of a scarf she'd tied
around her head like a lot of local women did to cover
their hair. She turned around to see the man she hadn't
been able to erase from her thoughts, standing there
in jeans and a jacket. He looked too marvelous to her
this early in the morning.

"I wanted to slip out before your mother awakened

so I wouldn't disturb her. I left messages to thank her and my aunt."

"I'm sure she'll appreciate that, Principessa."

Of course he'd recognized her and had talked with Lina. Now he knew everything about her situation. She was so sorry he'd been dragged into her problem. "Your mother has been exceptionally kind to me. I'm embarrassed my *zia* asked for her assistance, and I'm ashamed I accepted it because it has placed her in danger."

"Mamma has a big heart. It sounds like Signora Spadaro does, too."

Tears glazed her eyes. "They're both strong, remarkable women, but they've done more than enough to help me. It's time I dealt with the mess I've created for myself."

She tried to open the door, but it wouldn't give. Tuccia looked over her shoulder. "Is there a trick to unlocking it?"

With a half smile that gave her heart a jolt, he activated the remote in his hand and the door swung open.

"Thank you." After a slight hesitation, she said, "It was a privilege to meet the famous son of Lina Donati. In case you didn't know it, she thinks the sun rises and sets with you."

Tuccia felt him follow her out the door into the balmy seventy-seven-degree air where a limousine had pulled in the drive. She put on her sunglasses. Apparently he was going somewhere. When she would have walked past it, he called to her.

"Mamma says you need to get out of Palermo immediately. If you'll climb in the limo, I have the means to make that happen."

His comment stopped her in her tracks. "You mustn't get involved in my problem. I'm already weighed down with guilt and couldn't handle any more."

He opened the rear door. "But I *am* involved. I don't believe I've ever helped a genuine princess in distress before and rather like the idea. Come on. You've been living dangerously since leaving Paris. Why stop now?"

His sense of humor caught her off guard and she chuckled in spite of the fear gripping her that this freedom couldn't last. Not wanting to hold things up, she climbed in. He set her suitcase on the bank of seats in front of them and sat next to her, pulling the door shut. His rock-hard limbs brushed against her jeans-clad legs. The contact sent a dart of awareness through her body.

She heard him tell the chauffeur to drive them to the airport. They drove through a breathtaking portion of Mondello to the main route leading out of the city. Tuccia had the sensation of being spirited away where nothing could hurt her.

It was a heavenly feeling she'd never experienced before. She'd sell her soul for it to last, but she knew this wonderful moment could only be enjoyed until they reached the airport.

"Where are we going?" she asked at last, alive to everything about this extraordinary man.

"To Milan."

"Where you work when you're not in New York."

"More importantly, it's where you'll be safe. I fear my mother has done far too much talking about me."

"That's because she loves you." Tuccia had heard about the spectacular *castello* restaurant he owned and ran with his business partners. His other business interests in New York City were legendary. "I can't imagine what it would be like to know that kind of love from my own parents."

"That's a lonely statement."

"Now *I'm* doing too much talking and sound so sorry for myself, I'm ashamed. But you have no idea what I'd give to erase the image the country has of me. I'm *not* the tempestuous, volatile woman everyone believes me to be. I just want to be free like other women to make the kind of life I want for myself."

"According to my mother, you've run away from a fate worse than death."

"Put that way it sounds ridiculous, doesn't it? Unfortunately it's true for me and I've dragged three innocent people into my personal disaster. I pray there won't be any repercussions for you," she half sobbed the words.

His hand grasped hers, sending a wave of warmth through her. "No one brought my mother and me kicking and screaming," he teased gently. "If I were in your shoes and betrothed to some odious *marchesa* twice my age, I can promise you I would flee to the other side of the universe where no one would ever find me."

Odious was the exact word to describe Jean-Michel.

The analogy was so ludicrous she found herself laughing. But it underlined the fact that Cesare Donati wasn't married. Tuccia couldn't help but wonder how many women must have flung themselves at him.

"That's better," he said before releasing her hand.

Soon they arrived at the airport and were driven to

the area where the private jets sat on the tarmac. The limo wound around and stopped next to one in silver and blue that stood out with a coat of arms depicting the Duc di Lombardi. A thrill of excitement passed through her to know she'd be flying to northern Italy with him. Just the two of them.

Once Cesare helped her out of the limo with her suitcase, the steward welcomed them aboard. He showed her to the elegant club compartment where she sat across from her protector as she thought of him. Pretty soon the Fasten Seat Belt light went on and she heard the scream of the engines as they taxied out to the runway.

After they'd taken off and achieved cruising speed, the light went off and the steward brought them breakfast trays. She found she was starving and ate everything, including a second cup of coffee to drink.

Cesare flashed her a searching glance. "How long has it been since you had a substantial meal?"

"My aunt kept trying to feed me after I arrived in Palermo, but I was so nervous I couldn't eat very much. Now I'm hungry."

"How did you manage your escape so perfectly when all of your other attempts have failed?"

"I can see my aunt has told your mother everything about my past." Tuccia heaved a sigh. "I've been planning this latest scheme since my first dress fitting two months ago. Yesterday morning I went to the dressmaker with my mother for the final wedding dress fitting.

"When Madame Dufy went to find the dressmaker and bring out my gown, I told my mother I needed to use the ladies' room and hurried down the hallway. As

soon as no one was in sight, I shot out the back door
of the salon. I knew there was a nearby *tête de taxi*.
From there I was driven to the airport where Bertina
had chartered a private jet for me ahead of time under
a fake name. And here I am."

His gaze held hers. "That was a daring plan."

"I'm sure you think me selfish and cruel, but it
was the only way to end the nightmare of my life.
I've written a letter to Jean-Michel to apologize. It's
all ready to be mailed except for a stamp."

"Where is it?"

"In my purse."

"May I see it?"

When she pulled it out, he walked over and took
it from her. After examining the address, he put it in
his pocket. "I'll make sure he gets it without the police being able to trace it."

"You must think me heartless and that I'm living
up to all the falsehoods spread about me. Actually
they're not all false. I do have a bad temper that erupts
at times and I've gotten a lot of staff into trouble who
were supposed to keep a close watch on me."

After a silence he said, "What I think doesn't matter." The Fasten Seat Belt light went on again. He
strapped himself in. "We're descending to Milan.
Very soon I'll take you to a place where you'll be
hidden from the world and hopefully safe for another twenty-four hours. While you're figuring out
what it is you would like to do with the rest of your
life, I'll have to leave you, but I'll be back in a couple of days."

Her spirits plunged at that revelation. "Where are
you going?"

"To Palermo."

"Again? I don't understand."

"I'm going to see the man I'd hired to be the *castello*'s new executive pastry chef."

Her brows met in a delicate frown. "Why didn't you visit with him before you brought me all this way first?"

The pilot set the jet down and it taxied to a stop. "Because he was rushed to the hospital during the night and couldn't come with me to start his new position. He was supposed to meet my partners today and get settled in."

"Oh, how terrible for him *and* you!"

"Since you needed to leave Palermo before the authorities caught up to you, I brought you instead."

The man continued to astound her. She shook her head. "I can't believe you would do that for me." Tuccia loved him already for his sacrifice.

His blue eyes darkened with an emotion she couldn't put her finger on. "Mamma said it was a matter of life and death. After learning how desperate you are to escape the life your parents and fiancé have orchestrated for you, I'm inclined to believe she was telling the truth."

His compassion filled her with feelings that threatened to overwhelm her. "Please—you don't have to send my letter to the *comte*. It's too much. I'll find a way to do it," she said in a throbbing voice he could probably feel.

"It's a simple thing that needs to be done so he'll call off his army. There's no one like you, and no question he wants you back. Needless to say, you're a royal prize he won't tolerate getting away from him."

Tuccia shivered because she felt he truly did understand the gravity of her desperate situation where Jean-Michel was involved.

A few minutes later another limousine drove them out of the city. They swept past farms and villas until they reached a small village at the base of a prominent hill. On the top she caught sight of a massive fortress. The ochre-toned structure with its towers and crenellated walls sprawled across the summit.

"That's the ancient Castello Di Lombardi," Cesare explained, "now a hotel *ristorante*."

The one he'd helped to make famous. Tuccia was eager to see it up close and thought they would drive up there. Instead he asked the driver to take them to a *pensione* in the village. Evidently he'd made arrangements for her ahead of time.

Just as he helped her out of the limo and told the driver to wait, the *padrona di casa* came out of another door. She greeted them and showed them inside the attractive apartment. After a few explanations she left. Cesare lowered Tuccia's suitcase to the floor and turned to her.

"You should be very comfortable here while I'm gone. I asked her to fill the cupboards and fridge with groceries to last several days. As you heard her say, if you need anything, just pick up the phone in the kitchen and she'll answer."

The last thing Tuccia wanted was for him to go, but she realized he was anxious to get back to Palermo and didn't dare keep him. What a terrible position he was in!

"I don't know how to thank you for all you've done for me. How can I make this up to you?"

He studied her features for a minute. "I've had two friends who helped me when I thought all was lost. It's nice to be on the giving end for a change."

She could feel her eyes smarting. "I don't deserve this."

"I remember telling them the same thing. A word of warning. Do you have a cell phone on you?"

"Yes."

"Don't use it for any reason and don't go walking in the village. The only person who knows you are here is the woman who let you in. She's a friend and will keep silent. When I return, we'll talk. Until then, try to relax, watch TV. *A presto*, Principessa."

"*Alla prossima*, Cesare." She followed him to the door and watched him drive away, causing her heart to act up until it actually hurt.

Once he was gone, Tuccia went back in the living room for her suitcase. Then she walked to the bedroom so full of emotions, she didn't know where to go with them. She didn't know another person in the world except her aunt who would make a sacrifice like this for her. Cesare Donati was the most incredible man she'd ever known.

While she was in the shower, her mind focused on the chef he'd hired for his fabulous *castello* restaurant. He had to be a spectacular cook. How sad he'd fallen ill at the very moment he was supposed to go to Milan with Cesare.

She wished she could help him in some way during the short interim while the chef was recovering. Cesare had been so good to her and she wanted to find a way to repay him. She'd much rather stay right here.

But of course the whole plan was to get her away from Jean-Michel and her parents.

You're losing your mind, Tuccia.

On his way back to the airport Cesare phoned his mother, wondering what kind of a mess she could be in if the police had already found out she'd been harboring Tuccia at the villa.

She picked up on the fourth ring. "Cesare—where are you?" she blurted before he could say anything.

"You'll be happy to know my mission has been accomplished. Are you alone?"

"Si."

"Good. Now I can tell you the princess has been installed in a safe place."

"Grazie a Dio. I can always count on you."

She didn't sound worried about the police yet. "I'm flying back to Palermo to be with you. If there are no complications, I should be there in about two hours. I'll come straight to the hospital. After we've talked to the doctor and done all we can do there, I'll take you out to eat and we'll have a long talk. How does that sound?"

"Wonderful, except that there's no point in your coming back unless you want me to help you find another pastry chef beyond Palermo. That could take months."

"What do you mean another chef? I don't understand. Ciro will get better with a treatment of antibiotics."

"I thought so, too, but *you're* not going to be happy when I tell you what I've just found out from the doctor. Ciro came close to dying during the night because he has developed a heart condition. The prognosis for a full recovery could be six months away."

"Incredibile!"

"I know how upset you must be to hear that news, Cesare. I'm so sorry. He's in the ICU and won't be able to talk to anyone for a few days. There'd be no point in your coming right now. You might as well turn around and stay at the *castello* until he's been given a private room and can have visitors. Then you can fly down and have a serious talk with him."

The situation had gone from bad to worse. "Thank you for watching over him. I'm indebted to you."

"Bless you for saving Tuccia's life. What will you do about the chef position now?"

Right now Cesare's concern over the princess had created the most stress for him. "That's not your problem. I'll just have to be the pastry chef myself and interview more applicants for the position. But let's agree that finding someone who knows how to make Sicilian desserts with an expertise close to his or yours will be an endeavor in futility."

"You make the best *cassatine* with almond paste in existence."

"I learned from you, but that was years ago."

"You never forget, but I'm desolate for you this has happened. What will Tuccia do? Did she talk to you about it during the flight?"

"Yes. She has a plan that might work." For a day maybe. "I'll think of something. Don't you worry about it. Have you told Bertina her niece is safe?"

"I drove to the palazzo to tell her in person and

give her Tuccia's letter before returning to the hospital. She was so relieved she broke down sobbing before burning it."

Good thinking on Bertina's part. "Have the police questioned her yet?"

"Yes. She told them she knew nothing."

"They'll be contacting anyone who is friends with her, especially her cook. You'll be receiving a visit soon. Don't talk to her on the phone."

"No worry. I'm at the hospital now and just finished reading Tuccia's sweet letter to me before burning it." He had a brilliant mother. "Thanks to your willingness to help the princess escape so fast, there's no evidence she was ever at the villa, and of course I know nothing." He chuckled in spite of his concern for her. "Stay in close touch with me."

"Haven't I always? Take care of yourself, Mamma."

"You, too. I'll talk to you later. *Dio di benedica*, Cesare."

After they hung up, he told the limo driver to take him to the main express mail outlet in Milan. Asking him to wait, he went in to have Tuccia's letter to the *comte* couriered overnight to Cesare's attorney. Rudy Goldman always spent this time of year at his retreat in Barbados. Inside the mailing envelope he put the following instructions.

Rudy.
Put a stamp on this and send it airmail immediately.
Many thanks,
Cesare.

His attorney was the soul of discretion and always did what he was told without question. When Cesare had addressed the mailing envelope, he paid the clerk who put it in the slot. Before long it would be on its way to Bridgetown. The *comte* needed to receive it ASAP. Cesare knew in his gut the other man would start a search for his fiancée.

She *was* a prize. No one knew that better than Cesare. His thoughts wandered. Not every man would be worthy of her love when she had an ancestry that had made her unique in the world. Certainly not Cesare, whose family tree might as well have half a trunk missing. What could a fatherless man bring to a marriage with a princess?

Depressed by his thoughts, he returned to the limo and told the driver to take him back to the *pensione*. It was the same apartment where Vincenzo's wife Gemma had once stayed when she'd come from Florence to the *castello* for an interview. The *padrona* could be trusted.

By the time the limo pulled up in front, Cesare had made up his mind to send Tuccia to the States in the morning. The police wouldn't find her there and he could put her out of his mind. She was on it too much already.

He got out to the pay the driver, then walked to the front door of her apartment and knocked loud enough for her to hear. "Tuccia? It's Cesare. May I come in?"

"You haven't left for Palermo yet?" she called out in surprise. "I'll be right there."

In less than a minute she opened the door in bare feet, dressed in the yellow silk robe she'd worn in the middle of the night. He could smell the peach shampoo she'd used to wash her hair. She had a brush in one hand and had been styling her naturally curly black hair.

The sight of such natural beauty would make any man go weak in the knees. Cesare was no exception. "I had a call from my mother and have been forced to change my plans."

"Uh-oh." Anxiety marred her features. He knew what she was thinking.

"Forgive me for making you stand there. Please come in."

Her faultless manners impressed him. "Thank you." He walked in the little living room off the kitchen.

She eyed him nervously. "Did the police interrogate her already? Is she in terrible trouble?" Tuccia put the hand not holding the brush to her heart. "Bertina should never have involved your mother and I shouldn't have listened to her."

"So far everything is all right. The police talked to your aunt who told them she knew nothing. I'm sure my mother will be next, but she'll have no information, either. They both received your letters."

"I'm so glad. Then why have you changed your plans? I don't understand. But before you tell me, let me get dressed. Please sit down. I'll only be a minute."

He chose the chair by the coffee table while she rushed to her bedroom. Cesare caught a fleeting glimpse of her long shapely legs beneath the flap of her robe before she disappeared. He was growing more enamored of her by the second.

How could it be that after all the years of working with attractive businesswomen, he found himself in trouble just being in her presence for a few hours total. Along with her attributes, her utter femininity blew him away. It was a good thing she'd be gone tomorrow so there'd be no temptation to spend any extra time with her.

CHAPTER THREE

IN NO TIME Tuccia reappeared wearing a pair of white slacks and sandals toned with a café-au-lait-and-white print short-sleeved top. She sat on the end of the couch with one leg tucked under her. "Tell me what's wrong."

"As you know, the Sicilian pastry chef I'd planned to hire is in the hospital. But there's no telling when he'll be well enough to work again. Mamma found out he has developed an unexpected heart condition. I had high hopes for him. With his exciting creations, he would have brought a new clientele to our *ristorante*. Except for my mother's cooking, there's no one to equal him."

Tuccia sat forward with a troubled look on her lovely face. "My *zia* says she's the most superb cook in all Sicily. That means she has to know what she is talking about. What will you do?"

"Since I'm in charge of the *ristorante* at the *castello*, I'm the only one who has the authority to fix the problem. In an emergency, there are times when you have to do it yourself."

Her eyes widened. "You mean *you're* going to be the pastry chef?"

"It'll be nothing new to me while I find someone else. But right now I'm concerned about you. Have you decided what you want to do with your life?"

A slow smile broke out on her face. "That was a trick question, right?"

The woman was getting to him. "Not at all. Since you never intended to follow through on the betrothal, what had you imagined you would be doing when you finally made your escape?"

Her smile faded. She looked away. "To be honest I only thought about how to subsist until my parents stopped looking for me and go from there."

Cesare had assumed as much. "If I hadn't offered you safe passage on the jet this morning, what was your exact plan when you reached Catania?"

"I was going to find temporary work in a greenhouse through an old school friend until I'm forced to move on for fear of being spotted."

He hadn't expected to hear that. "Are you a gardener with a knowledge of horticulture that would make you an asset at the greenhouse?"

"Of course not."

"Yet you're willing to prevail on the friend you mentioned to get a job there?"

"Yes. She works at the university and could help me find a position for a while. But because you told me not to use my phone, I haven't talked to her yet and wouldn't be able to until I reached Catania."

"Do you have an affinity for flowers?"

Her head flew back. "Have you forgotten I'm a princess who has no knowledge of anything practical? But I'm strong and could cart plants around in a wheelbarrow if I have to."

"I wasn't trying to insult you."

"I know," she half moaned. "You're being so good to me. I'm sorry I snapped."

"I think you're handling your desperate situation with amazing grace."

She shook her head. "But it's one I created and I don't deserve your kindness."

"Why do you say that? Everyone deserves help from time to time."

He heard a deep sigh. "I guess because my parents rarely showed any kindness to me while I was growing up."

"Did they hurt you physically?"

"Oh, no. Nothing like that. But their stifling, rigid rules made my life unbearable."

"Nevertheless it doesn't mean you're not deserving of kindness," he reminded her. "Just so you know, your letter to Jean-Michel has been dealt with in a way that won't be traced to you. He should be getting it in a few days, so you can put that worry out of your mind."

Her eyes filled with tears. "You're a saint."

"Hardly." He leaned toward her with his hands on his thighs. "I've given your precarious position a lot of thought. Your idea to go to Catania would only be a stopgap for a few days. I still think it would be best if you leave Europe tomorrow. I'll arrange it."

She shook her head. "I couldn't let you do that. You've done more than enough for me and have your own problem to solve right here."

"First things first, Tuccia. You need to get far away. New York would be the perfect place to get lost. With my contacts, I could set you up in your own apartment and they would help you find a job that you would like to do. No one would suspect you're the princess who disappeared. You'd be safe. That is what you want, isn't it?"

"You know it is, but I've been thinking about the chef who's in the hospital and how desperate you must be feeling right now. You saved my life by bringing me to Milan. Instead of putting you in an impossible position, I'd like to do something of value for you in return," she said in an aching voice.

She had a way of running over every roadblock. He sat back and studied her for a moment, intrigued. "What do you mean?"

"Why not teach me to be a pastry chef so I can work at your *ristorante* until he's well and can fly here. I'd do anything to help you if I could."

It took all his self-control not to laugh. To his shock, he had the strongest suspicion she was being completely serious. "Are you saying you know how to cook?"

A small sound escaped her throat. "No. I'm embarrassed to tell you I've never cooked anything from start to finish in my life, although I spent a lot of time in the palazzo kitchen growing up. The cooks were kind to me and let me watch. I washed lettuce and sometimes they'd let me beat egg whites or stir the gravy. Once in a while they'd allow me to sift the flour into the cake bowl before it was baked."

"Does that mean you didn't learn to cook at boarding school?"

She laughed outright. "You have a strange idea of what goes on there."

"Actually I *do* know, and was only teasing." Despite the impossibility of what she'd said, the more they talked, the more he found himself enjoying her company. Too much in fact.

"I'm relieved to hear it, Cesare. To be honest, that boarding school in France happened so long ago I've forgotten. All I know is, I was waited on. When my parents enrolled me at the University of Paris, I had to live with them in an apartment in St. Germain des Pres. Would it reassure you to know that I told my maid I could make my own tea and instant coffee in the microwave?"

He laughed at her sense of humor and her sparse knowledge in the cooking department. A princess with a classic education from the finest schools and universities in Europe, but to make a pastry... "Tuccia—"

"Please hear me out, Cesare," she cut him off before he could say anything else. "According to your mother, you could head any Cordon Bleu cooking school in the world. You could teach me. It would be like getting a college education of a different kind."

His eyes searched hers. She wasn't kidding. Princess Tuccianna had been known for doing some daring, outlandish things, but this idea had shocked him to the core.

"As intelligent and resourceful as you are, you don't know what would be entailed."

She sat forward. "My parents' cooks didn't know how to cook in the beginning, did they? They had to learn from someone," she reasoned. "Why couldn't I do the same thing under your expert tutelage? I'd work fast and it would free you up to get on with running all your businesses. My anonymity would be assured hidden behind the *castello* walls. Within six months, the chef you hired would be back."

Cesare no longer felt like laughing. This beautiful young woman was bargaining for her life. He had to give her credit for possessing the kind of guts he hadn't seen in most people.

When he didn't say anything, she blurted, "I've been thinking about what you asked me."

"What was that?"

"About what I wanted to do with my life. If you were to teach me how to make pastry, I would have learned a marketable skill. When Signor Fragala returns, I'd be able to use all that knowledge I'd learned from you. With a reference from you—provided you gave me a good one if I deserved it—I could find a position in any country."

He could hear her mind working. It was going like a house on fire. To his astonishment he was listening to her because she was making a strange kind of sense.

"After a half year in hiding, I'm positive my family will have disowned me so it wouldn't matter where I chose to live and work. I'd be a normal woman with a good job."

"You'll never be a normal woman, Principessa." his voice grated. Nor would he want her to be. He liked her exactly the way she was. "Can you honestly sit there and tell me the thought of being disowned doesn't pain you?"

She lowered her head. "I guess I don't know how I'd feel about it until it happened. But what I *do* know is that I'm *never* going to bow to my parents' wishes again. Hopefully before long Jean-Michel will have comforted himself with another mistress while he hunts for a new titled princess to marry."

Cesare rubbed the back of his neck, unable to believe he was actually toying with the idea of teaching her the rudiments. In a perfect world, if she did follow through and did learn how to cook, it would give her the independence she'd never known. It would allow her to earn money and she'd be free to make her own choices, something that had been denied her from birth.

At some point in time she'd decide to get in touch with her parents, or not. He couldn't believe he was allowing his thoughts to go this far.

Quiet reigned before she said, "I know what you're thinking. I don't have any money right now to pay you to teach me. But if I were a good student and could work at the *castello*, you wouldn't have to pay me any money. Not ever! I'm already indebted to you for your sacrifice. It would be my gift to you for saving my life."

The last was said in a trembling voice. It was the wobble that did it to him.

"Are you a fast learner?" Cesare knew she was grateful. He didn't want her to go on begging for the chance to repay him. Her willingness to take a risk of these proportions made her a breed apart from anyone he'd ever known.

She stared at him with those heavenly gray eyes. "I guess that depends on the subject matter, but I graduated with honors in European history."

"Congratulations, Tuccia. That's no small feat. But to make a pastry chef out of you... I don't know."

"You're right. It's too much to ask and I'd probably be a disaster."

He didn't like the discouraged tone of her voice and it made up his mind for him. "Maybe not."

A gasp escaped her lips. "You mean you're willing to entertain the idea?"

Her excitement put a stranglehold on him. "Let's just say I'll put you on probation for a few days and see how it goes."

"You're not teasing me?" she cried.

"No. I wouldn't do that. Not about this."

He could tell she was fighting tears. "When would I start?"

"As soon as we've eaten dinner."

"So soon? Aren't you exhausted after everything you've been through in the last twenty-four hours?"

Her question stunned him because her first thought had been for him. He could have asked the same of her after being on the run.

"Not at all." In fact he'd never been so wired in his life.

"Does that mean we're going up to the *castello* right now?"

He stood up. "No. This *pensione* is going to be your home, your school room and your lab. You'll do everything hands-on right here. After a few days I'll decide if I can turn you into the next executive pastry chef at the Castello Supremo Hotel and Ristorante di Lombardi. Otherwise I'll put you on the plane for New York."

Tuccia let out an incredulous cry of joy and she jumped to her feet. She rushed over to him and put a hand on his arm. The contact sent a shock through him. His awareness of her made it hard to breathe.

"You mean it? You're not joking? But you just said you weren't joking. I'm sorry, but I just can't believe you're willing to give me a chance."

"Everyone deserves a chance." He looked her in the eye, trying to get a grip on his emotions. "What fake name were you going to use when you applied for the greenhouse job in Catania?"

His question made her blink, and she let go of him. "Come on," he prodded her. "You've obviously had one in mind for a long time."

"Not the same one my *zia* used to charter that plane for me. I guess... Nedda Bottaro."

"Nedda? The heroine in the opera *Pagliacci*?"

"Yes. I love opera and *Pagliacci* is one of my favorites."

"But Nedda meets such a cruel end."

"I know. She and Carmen suffered the same fate. I always cry."

Cesare heard pain in her voice. "Why use the last name Bottaro?"

"It means a wine cask maker. There'd be no connection to any of my family names."

He nodded. "Wise decision. If I deem you a promising pupil, we'll go with both when I introduce you to my partners. I'll tell them I stole you from the finest *ristorante* in Palermo."

She rubbed her hands against womanly hips in a nervous gesture. "How soon will that happen?"

"Not for a while. I'll have to teach you a lot first, and quickly, too. After dinner we'll start with something simple. I'll take a taxi to the grocery store and get the needed ingredients. While I'm at it, I'll buy you a new Pay as You Go phone to reach me if you need to and program it. By the time you go to bed, you'll be able to make the recipe I have in mind in your sleep."

She paced the floor, then wheeled around in front of him. "If I can pass your tests, that means I'll be making desserts for hundreds of people a week."

"That's right. Kings, sheikhs, presidents of countries."

Her radiating smile illuminated those hidden places in his soul that had never seen light. That thought appeared to delight her.

"You'll have assistants to help you."

"But I don't look anything like a chef."

No. She didn't look like anyone else in the whole wide world. "You will after we dress you properly. When I bring my partners to the kitchen to introduce you, no one will ever guess you're Princess Tuccianna."

Her cheeks had grown becomingly flushed. "I want to be good enough to meet your standards. You'll never know what this means to me."

He was beginning to. While she stood there, Cesare phoned for a taxi. After he hung up, he turned to her. "I'm starving and am going out to pick up a meal for us after I shop. When I get back, we'll get started."

She followed him to the door. "If I can't do the job you need done, does this mean you'll have to be the head pastry chef at your own hotel?"

He liked it that she was a little worried about him. "Yes. My partner's wife, Gemma, can no longer handle the job this late in her pregnancy. I'd promised I would produce her replacement by tomorrow, but with Signor Fragala in the hospital, the job has now fallen on my shoulders. I'll have to let them know in the morning. That doesn't give me time to find anyone else with his credentials. It could take me several months."

"And I don't have *any*," she half moaned the words.

In an unconscious gesture he put a hand on her shoulder and kneaded it gently. "I'm not my mother's son for nothing. You've convinced me you want this job more than anything. By the time I'm through with you, I'm hoping you'll be able to write your own ticket as a pastry chef."

After a long pause he said, "At this point I've been wondering. Is the difficult, uncontrollable, incorrigible Principessa di Trabia of Palermo, Sicily, worth her salt? It would be fun to find out the truth. I'll be back soon."

Tuccia rested against the closed door with her arms folded. His touch had crept through her body like a fine wine, weakening her physically. Yet his final comment before he'd gone out the door had caused a sudden surge of adrenaline to attack her.

"Is the difficult, uncontrollable, incorrigible Principessa di Trabia of Palermo, Sicily, worth her salt?"

Cesare had said that to get a rise out of her. Without question he'd accomplished his objective.

Frightened and excited by the whole situation she'd created for herself, Tuccia turned on the TV in the corner to distract her for a little while. She grazed the channels with the remote and came across two stations giving the four o'clock news. The second she saw a news clip of herself and Jean-Michel flash on the screen, she felt sick and sank down on the couch.

"Authorities in France and Italy are asking for anyone to come forward who knows anything about the whereabouts of Princess Tuccianna of Sicily, the daughter of the Marchese and Marchesa di Trabia. She's the fiancée of the acting Comte Jean-Michel Ardois of the House of Ardois and prominent CEO of Ardois Munitions. Princess Tuccianna disappeared yesterday morning in Paris and hasn't been seen since.

"The famous couple were to have been married today. Speculation that she was kidnapped by some foreign government faction for ransom has not been counted out.

"According to police, the Marchesa had been waiting in the lounge for her daughter to change after the final fitting of her wedding gown at the exclusive bridal shop on the Rue de L'Echelle. But she never came out. The police found her betrothal ring and are suspicious that some employees working at the shop helped aid in the kidnapping and are now being detained.

"Both families are desperate for news of the beautiful dark-haired twenty-five-year-old princess. So far any sightings of her have turned out to be false. She speaks French, Spanish, English, Italian, Sicilian and is known to be an excellent swimmer and sailor who—"

Tuccia turned off the TV and buried her face in her hands, swamped by guilt for the terrible thing she'd done. At least Jean-Michel would get her letter soon, but in the meantime innocent people were being questioned and detained. Hundreds of policemen in two countries were searching for her. She'd endangered her aunt and Cesare's mother. But she couldn't go back to that life. She just couldn't.

Jean-Michel wanted to marry a woman with a title, preferably a young one who'd give him children and not cause him trouble. Her parents wanted a son-in-law with a fortune that would never run out. No love was involved. Tuccia was a pawn and always had been. It was a fact of life that she'd been born to royalty.

It truly wasn't fair to Cesare, who'd been forced to come to her rescue this morning, flying her with him on the ducal jet no less. Knowing the huge risk of aiding a fugitive—that's what she was at this point—a lesser man might never have done such a favor, not even for his own mother.

To add to her crime, Tuccia had proposed an idea to save both their skins. But it was so audacious *and* dangerous if anyone were to find out who she was. For Cesare to be willing to go along with her idea made him a prince among men as far as she was concerned.

He had a reputation for being brilliant. She'd known that about Lina's son long before she'd ever met him. But she hadn't counted on him being so incredibly handsome, too. Working with him, she would fast lose her objectivity. How could she possibly concentrate on what she was doing while she was in his presence? If there was such a thing as love at first sight, she'd fallen victim to it.

By working with him, there was no doubt she'd be learning from a master. It would be an honor to be the student of a man famous on two continents for his business acumen as a restaurateur. He'd built an enviable empire of restaurants in New York.

Part of her wanted to show him she *was* worth her salt. But what if she failed? She'd passed lots of tests in her life, but none would be more important than this one now that she'd made the commitment.

While she was sorting through her tortured thoughts she heard a knock on the door. Tuccia rushed to let him in. He was loaded with three big sacks of food and carried them into the kitchen.

She shut the door behind him. "It looks like you bought out the store."

"Several stores to be exact." He washed his hands in the sink. "The risotto with veal looked good at the deli. I picked up some rustic wheat bread and a bottle of Chardonnay Piemonte to go with it."

"Wonderful. I'm hungry, too." She peeked in the sacks and found their dinner, which she put on the round kitchen table. Their gazes fused. "I take it the other two sacks contain enough pastry ingredients to feed a small army."

"You're partially right. The rest are provisions for you to take with you in case you change your mind before the evening is over."

Her spirits plunged. "What do you mean?"

"While I've been gone, you've had time to reconsider what we've talked about. After we've eaten, I'll be happy to take you to the train station if that's your wish. The standard service leaves at quarter to nine for Sicily. There'll be no amenities. You'll have to sit up in your seat all night. But you'll be like dozens of passengers with little money and melt into the crowd."

He pulled wine glasses from the cupboard and poured some for them, but what he'd just said to her had shocked her.

CHAPTER FOUR

TUCCIA STOOD THERE with her hands on her hips. "You honestly expected that I would change my mind while you were gone? That I didn't mean any of the things I said?"

"It would be understandable," he said, sounding so reasonable she wanted to scream.

"Naturally you have every right to believe I'm not up to the task. No one would believe it."

"I have faith in you, but I want to give you the freedom to back out of this if you think you might have spoken too hastily."

As they sat down to eat, he handed her a copy of the *Il Giorno* newspaper to read. She came face-to-face with a two-month-old picture of her and Jean-Michel attending the opera in Paris. The headline read, *Sicilian Princess still missing*.

"You've done a good job of disappearing, Tuccia. So good I believe you have an excellent chance to reach Catania unobserved with your disguise. I had no right to suggest you go to New York. You're a grown woman and can make your decisions. It's time you were allowed to function without interference from anyone."

He ate a second helping of veal. The minutes were ticking away. Maybe he was wishing she would leave for Catania, then he'd never have to give her another thought in his life.

Her appalling selfishness sickened her. She couldn't help but wonder if he was disgusted with the overindulged princess who'd created an international incident. He'd have every right!

It was miraculous he'd let his mother talk him into bringing her to Milan, except that Tuccia's aunt was a force to contend with. Because his mother worked for Bertina, she probably didn't know how to say no to her.

Unable to handle her own ugly thoughts any longer, she got to her feet and clung to the back of the chair. He looked at her while he finished off the bread.

"Cesare?" she began.

"Yes?"

"When I was at your mother's last night, I was frightened out of my wits at what I'd done to escape my prison. Terrified would be a better word. That is until this morning, when you snatched me away from the jaws of death at great risk. I know that sounds dramatic, but that's how it felt to me and still does."

"I have no doubt of it."

She struggled to say the rest. "You've saved my life. If you're really willing to teach me how to make pastry, and you think I can learn, I'd like to try. I want to help you honor your commitment to your partners who are depending on you. I haven't changed my mind about any of it. But if the police don't find me first, I can only pray your friends won't discover I'm a fraud who has made a mess of everything for you."

The blue of his eyes darkened as they stared at her out of dark-fringed lashes. The male beauty of the man caused her to feel desire for him even to the palms of her hands.

"I believe you. No matter how you see yourself, Tuccia, in my opinion you're the bravest woman I ever met and I believe you can take the challenge head-on," he said in a husky tone. "What brought you to this decision?"

After the unexpected compliment, Tuccia had difficulty swallowing. "I couldn't let you get away with thinking I'm not worth my salt."

There was a gleam in his eyes. "I'm impressed by your willingness to put yourself in the hands of a stranger."

"That part is easy, Cesare. Because I've been friends with your mother, you haven't been a stranger to me, even if we didn't meet until last night." She was embarrassed because she could hear the throb in her voice. All it had taken was meeting him to be crazy about him.

He got to his feet and started clearing the table. "She likes you enough to have begged me to help you escape. That shows the strength of your friendship. It's good enough for me."

"I'm just sorry I'm the clay you have to work with to try and make a pastry cook out of me. But I swear I'll work my hardest for you."

"You've convinced me. Shall we get busy?"

"Yes. What will we make first?"

"The most clamored-for dessert in Sicily. I'm sure you've eaten virgin breasts before."

Tuccia should have been ready for that one, but it

was so unexpected heat scorched her cheeks. She went over to the sink to wash her hands. "You can't be a Sicilian without having eaten those cakes. But when I was little, the cook at the palazzo was offended by their name so she called them nun buns."

A chuckle escaped his lips. "They have several names. Mamma grew up in an orphanage run by the nuns," he continued. "They were known for being great cooks and made those special delicacies for which they're famous. She taught me everything she learned from them. Tonight we'll get started on the first of three different kinds."

"I didn't know there was more than one."

"You'd be surprised at the varieties."

She knew he was talking about the cakes, but her blush deepened anyway.

"Some of the ingredients have to be refrigerated before completing them, but we'll finish everything before you have to go bed. In a few days' time we'll present them to my partners as your specialty when I introduce you. A bite into them and they'll believe they'd been transported to heaven."

Laughter peeled out of her. "I hope you're right!"

His laughter filled the kitchen. "Why don't you sit down and we'll go over the recipe. It's known only to my mother and me." He walked over to one of the sacks and pulled out a notebook and pen. She shouldn't have been surprised all that knowledge was etched in his brain.

"Shall I write it down while you dictate?" she asked as he handed her the items.

"I think that would be best for you. To read your own writing rather than try to figure out mine will save you time in the long run. That notebook is going to be your bible. Don't ever lose it. Are you ready?"

"Yes," she said in a tentative voice.

Last night Tuccia had appeared to Cesare like a fantastic female apparition that had made him think maybe he was hallucinating. This evening she wasn't just a heavenly face and body. In the last eighteen hours she'd taken on substance and exhibited a keen intellect that had been growing on him by the minute.

In her desperation to remain hidden from the world for a while, she'd begged him to teach her. He knew she was frightened. This woman, who'd been raised to be a princess, was running on faith.

Right now she reminded him of a young child, submissive and obedient to her parent. Cesare was humbled by her determination to grab the lifeline he'd thrown her. He'd brought the newspaper with him to help remind her that anything—even learning how to cook pastry—was better than being forced to go back to her old life.

"The first item you'll be making is called *pasta frolla* for the shells. These are the ingredients: four cups of flour, one cup of granulated sugar, two sticks of sweet butter, one tablespoon of honey, five medium egg yolks, lightly beaten, and lemon zest. After you've kneaded it and put it in the fridge for an hour, you'll make the ricotta cream filling. That requires one cup of sugar, two pounds of ricotta, orange zest, cinnamon powder, one drop of vanilla, a quarter pound of candied citron and chocolate shavings to taste. Lemon glacé will be the final step that includes one and a half cups of granulated sugar, a quarter cup of lemon juice, and a sprinkle of raspberries. I realize this sounds like a lot, but it's straightforward. You'll like forming the shells. Are you with me so far?"

She looked up with a faint smile. "Yes. I can't wait to find out if I share your optimism."

Her response was encouraging. "Come on. We'll get started on the dough. While you find us a bowl in the cupboard, I'll put the first set of ingredients on the table."

He oversaw everything, but made her do all the work. She added the ingredients, making little mistakes, but soon she'd formed it into a ball.

"Okay. Now knead it."

"I know how to do that from watching the cook." But once she got started, the dough kept sticking to her fingers. "This is impossible!" she cried in frustration.

Cesare burst into laughter. "Wash your hands, and then dust them with flour before trying it again."

"But that will wash half the dough away."

"No problem."

"That's what you say," she mumbled, but did his bidding and started over with the kneading. "This is much better." She finally lifted her head and smiled. "Thank you."

"You're welcome. Now pat it into a disk and wrap it in wax paper. An hour in the fridge and it will be ready to shape into tart shells. While the dough is getting cold, you'll start making the filling."

Three hours and three tries later she'd produced a pan of tarts she was willing to let him taste. After she'd decorated them with the lemon glacé, she designed the tops in an artful way with raspberries and chocolate shavings.

With a hand he could tell was trembling, she put one on a dish and handed it to him. "Will you be the first to sample my *pièce de resistance*?"

Cesare knew what this moment meant to her and he bit into it. She'd followed the recipe to the letter. He found no fault with the taste or texture and was so proud of her effort after three tries that he wanted to sweep her in his arms. Instead he kissed her hot cheek.

"Congratulations, Tuccia. My partners will tell you these tarts are perfect." He swallowed the whole thing and had to be careful not to swallow her, too.

"Thank you. I know they're anything but. The shells are still uneven and in this batch I put a little too much cinnamon in the filling when I tasted it."

"The fact that you know what you can improve on makes you an excellent cook already. How does it feel to have made a masterpiece created by the nuns?"

She took a deep breath. "If these tarts meet your exacting criteria, it's because you were my teacher. To answer your specific question, after I got over being nervous with you standing there watching me, I had more fun than I would have expected."

"Good. I'm glad to hear it."

"It amazes me that I've eaten desserts of every kind all my life and never paid attention to the intricacies that go into the preparation. That's what frightens me. This was just one dessert. When I think of the dozen others I have to learn how to make, I feel totally inadequate."

"Keep in mind that all it takes is one step at a

time. I'll wrap up your pan of mounds and take them with me."

"Why?"

"I want my partners to try them." He heard her groan. "After the dishes are done, I'll say good-night."

While he called for a limo, he watched how hard she worked to clean up the flour on the table and floor, let alone her clothes. She'd proved she was worth her salt, but this had only been her first lesson. Another few days of this and the last thing she would tell him was that it was fun.

He had to give her full marks for putting the kitchen back together with little help from him. "You've done a great job, Tuccia. I'll be back in the morning and we'll talk about what's going to happen. I hope you get a good sleep."

She walked him to the front door. "I'll never be able to thank you enough for shielding me and giving me this chance."

"I'm equally grateful and impressed that you're willing to try something so different from the world you've come from to help me. Who knows? We may pull this off yet."

She flashed him a tired smile. "'May' being the operative word. *Bona notti*," she called to him.

On Cesare's way to the *castello*, her parting words resonated inside him. She'd said good-night to him in Sicilian, using the Palermo dialect. It reminded him of the language he used with his own family, making him feel more connected to the princess.

That was bad. He couldn't afford to have intimate thoughts about her, but that was a joke because he could still feel her body pressed against his in his mother's kitchen. That was a moment he couldn't forget if he wanted to, even if she'd just run away from her fiancé.

Cesare had offered to help her so she could gain her independence. He hadn't done it to take advantage of her. The last thing he intended was to come on to her. If he did that, he'd be every bit as bad as the lecherous *comte* Cesare's mother had described.

You are just as bad, Donati.

By the time the limo dropped him off around the back of the *castello*, he realized he had to tell his partners the truth about her. If they couldn't handle it—and he was pretty sure they couldn't—he would understand. So would Tuccia. Even though he hadn't been around her long, he knew she'd pretend it was all right.

It was five to ten when he stole through the passageway to the back stairs not used by the hotel clientele. Halfway to his room on the second floor in the private section, he ran into Takis coming down the stairs from the turret bedroom he and Lys used when they were in Milan. They had their own home in Crete and flew back and forth.

"Cesare—You're back! We didn't expect to see you until tomorrow. What have you got there?"

"You'd be surprised."

Takis frowned. "What's going on?"

"I had a slight change in plans. Where are you headed?"

"To the kitchen." Takis smiled. "Lys had a sudden craving for ice cream."

"So it's true about pregnant women."

"*Si.* One day it'll be your turn to find out."

A sudden vision of a pregnant Tuccia in her yellow silk robe flashed through Cesare's mind, disturbing him.

"*Eh, amico.* What's wrong?"

Diavolo. What wasn't? "Everything's fine."

"The hell it is." Takis could read him like a book.

"Your wife needs you. Is Vincenzo here or in Lake Como with Gemma?"

"In order for us to be together tomorrow and meet the new cook, they never left for home."

"*Perfetto.* See you two in the morning."

Not wanting to prolong this any longer, Cesare bounded up the rest of the stairs. When he reached his suite, he put the tray of tarts on the coffee table and went in the other room to take a shower.

Later, after throwing on a robe, he phoned his mother and found out the police had been by the villa asking questions about Tuccia.

"I said I didn't know what they were talking about. I'd been at the hospital all day and told them to check the nursing station at San Giovanni if they needed verification. That was enough for them and they left. I'm positive they won't be back."

"*Grazie al cielo.*"

"Bertina is overjoyed no one can find her niece."

It might interest his mother to know Cesare's relief was just as great. The more he thought about Tuccia's detestable royal engagement, the happier he was that he'd played a part in her escape. As for the rest… "I take it Ciro is still in the ICU."

"Oh, yes. The nurse told me she would call me

when they moved him to a private room so I could visit."

"That's good."

"Tell me how you are. How's Tuccia?"

"We're both fine." He'd told Takis the same thing. Fine covered a lot of territory, good and bad. "Don't worry about anything. Get some sleep, Mamma. That's what I'm going to do."

Not wanting to answer any more questions, he hung up wondering if he'd be able to get any while he was torn apart by thoughts of Tuccia and what would be the best thing for her. Now that he'd agreed to help her, he had to see this through one way or the other. But he couldn't seem to stop from touching her. Earlier tonight he'd kissed her.

Cesare was about to turn out the overhead light when there was a knock on the door. Instinct told him it was Takis. He crossed the room and opened it to discover both him and Vincenzo standing at the threshold.

"Shouldn't you two be with your wives?"

Vincenzo's silvery stare had a way of pinning you in place. "We think you need us more."

"I'd hoped to have this conversation in the morning."

Takis shook his head. "Let's talk now or none of us will get any sleep."

How true. But the fear that his partners might not be on board with his plan to train Tuccia had been bothering him. Deep inside lurked another fear that if she left Milan to do something else, she wouldn't tell him where she'd gone and he might never see her again.

"Come in." They walked in his sitting room and sat down. He paced for a minute before coming to a stop. "I don't want to keep you up all night, so here's the bottom line. The person I'd hired for our *ristorante* is in the hospital in Palermo as we speak."

In the next breath Cesare explained everything that had happened from the moment he'd arrived at his mother's villa until now. He told them about Ciro's sudden illness and Tuccia's plight.

"I took her to the *pensione* where Gemma stayed. She's safe there for the time being. During the flight I came up with a solution to both problems."

In the next breath he told them of his idea to turn her into the temporary new pastry cook for the *castello* until Ciro was well. He only left two things out; the fact that she'd been the one who'd begged *him* for the job, and his intense attraction to the *principessa*. Cesare had never burned for a woman like this in his life.

"Hearing about her disappearance is like a dose of déjà vu for me," Vincenzo commented.

Cesare nodded. "When Mamma admitted why she was hiding Tuccia, I could understand. It took me back to that morning in New York when you told me and Takis about your escape from your father at eighteen years of age. She's twenty-five, but still in much the same situation as you were back then."

"That was a horrific time. I can well imagine what Princess Tuccianna is going through right now."

"But she's my responsibility, not yours. Tonight on the way up here I decided I had to be out of my mind to think up such a ridiculous plan." She'd been so desperate, he hadn't been able to find the strength to turn her down. "On the jet she talked about another plan she had in mind to stay in hiding. I don't doubt it would work for a while.

"Once she's gone I'll be acting pastry chef while I search for the right person to replace Gemma. I can only hope Ciro might recover much sooner than the doctor estimated."

Without commenting, Takis eyed the covered pan on the coffee table. "Are you going to let us taste her first endeavor?"

"I was just going to ask the same thing," Vincenzo commented.

"There's no point. I'm not willing to drag you two into this mess."

"Why don't you let us decide."

"No, Takis." He shook his head. "All we would need is for the press to find out she's working within the walls of the *castello*. We'd be charged for obstructing a police investigation. I'd face an additional charge for flying her here. It would cause an international scandal that could ruin our business."

At this point Vincenzo had gotten to his feet. "Not showing up for her wedding would be a disappointment to her fiancé and parents, but it isn't a crime. As far as I can see, no crime has been committed by anyone. She turned to her aunt for assistance. That woman called on your mother who enlisted your help. The police don't know that."

"Vincenzo's right," Takis chimed in. "Besides, Tuccia is over twenty-one and is welcome here as a staff worker. If she wore a disguise and used a fake name, it's not our fault we didn't recognize her."

"Thanks, guys, but the police wouldn't see any of it that way."

"How are they going to find out?"

Cesare rubbed the back of his neck in frustration. "I don't know, but you can be sure there'll be a leak somewhere."

Takis looked up at Cesare. "Mind if we find out what a good teacher you are?"

"Go ahead. She's never cooked anything in her life, but she followed Mamma's sacred recipe for Sicilian nun buns to the letter." He uncovered the pan so they could take one.

Both men started eating and didn't stop until half of the decorated mounds were gone. Tuccia could have received no greater compliment.

Vincenzo lifted his head. "You swear you didn't cook these yourself?"

"I stood over her shoulder. That's all."

"She really made these on her own?" Takis looked astounded.

Cesare nodded. "It took her three tries. She even cleaned up the mess in the kitchen afterwards."

"Do you think this was a one-time accident, or is the princess the proverbial diamond in the rough?"

"I'd like to see her make half a dozen Sicilian desserts at the *pensione* before I could answer that question, Takis. Today it was fear that drove her. She'd do anything to stay hidden. But to master the art of fine pastry making and love to do it is a gift only a few people possess. Within a few days she could hate it.

"As for her working here as the pastry chef, it would mean dealing with the kitchen assistants. I have no idea how she would handle them under pressure. For all of those reasons I'm going to tell her this won't work."

"Not so fast," Vincenzo interjected. "Before you say or do anything, why don't I ask Gemma to visit her tomorrow? Let her lay out what a day in the kitchen would be like for Tuccia. She'd be able to ask my wife questions about the routine and the personalities she would have to deal with."

"But Vincenzo—Gemma learned from her mother and studied pastry making for ten years at the finest school in Florence. She would laugh in disbelief at such a ludicrous idea."

Vincenzo shook his head. "We've all heard the news about the princess who ran away. No one would be more understanding than my wife who saw first-hand what went on between my father and me years ago. Takis and I agree those nun buns the princess made were divine. I think it's worth going to the trouble to give her a chance. I know Gemma will feel the same way."

"You don't want her on her feet at this late date in her pregnancy. Neither do I."

"Cooking for hours every day is entirely different than having a serious talk with Tuccia."

Takis nodded. "He's got a point, Cesare."

"I don't know. I have a lot to think about. Tomorrow when I go down to the *pensione*, I'll probably discover she wants to leave. Whatever is decided, I'll let you know. I guess you realize I'm indebted to you two for being the best friends any man could ever have. Now go to bed. That's an order."

Both men stole the rest of the mounds from the pan before walking out the door.

Cesare tossed and turned all night, too eager to see her again to sleep. Early the next morning he got dressed and left the *castello* in his hard-top sports car parked around the rear. He took the empty pan with him.

When he reached the village, he stopped at a *trattoria* for takeout: breakfast for two. To his dismay he realized that he was so excited at the prospect of seeing her again he couldn't think about anything else. Though it had only been a few days, Tuccia had taken up space in his mind and heart.

He'd known desire for women and had enjoyed several short-term relationships, but they'd always stopped short of marriage because some crucial element had been missing. That was what he'd always told himself. But this was different because so far Tuccia appealed to him on every level and had already colored his world.

He reached the *pensione* at eight and got out of the car. After knocking on the door, he expected her to answer in tears and be anxious to get to the train station.

CHAPTER FIVE

Last night Tuccia had wished Cesare had stayed. But if she'd asked him not to go, she would have given him the wrong idea. She had a problem because she knew she'd fallen in love with him and was more attracted to him with every passing minute. When the limo pulled away, she'd closed and locked the door, fearing she wouldn't get to sleep for a long time.

At four this morning, an exhausted Tuccia had turned off her watch alarm and got out of bed to do her homework. It was one thing to cook while Cesare had stood there directing her every step. The trick was to do it while he wasn't watching.

She knew there were enough ingredients for her to make one more batch of the tarts on her own. But with no big shallow pan, she'd had to improvise with two small round pans with higher sides she'd found in the cupboard. As a result, she still had half the batter to cook.

If she failed miserably, then she'd be the first to ask him to drive her to the train station. It would be the last thing he would ever have to do for her. Before she threw herself at him, she realized it would be better if she never saw him again.

Tuccia had thought her initial physical attraction to him would fade, but the opposite had happened. His underlying goodness as a human being had opened her eyes to the other qualities in his nature that had nothing to do with his striking male looks. Everything about him from his intellect to his humor stimulated her. So much, in fact, that she was breathless as she waited to see him again today.

The knock on the door came sooner than she had expected, sending her pulse racing as if she had a sickness. She put down the cup she'd been using to add the final lemon glaze to the tarts she'd made. There were still three to be coated and decorated.

After wiping her hands on a towel, she hurried to answer the door, knowing flour still dusted part of the same blouse she'd worn last evening. There was even some on her forearms.

When she opened it, their eyes met for a quiet moment. His were smiling, if there was such a thing. She got a fluttering in her chest as his gaze wandered over her.

"I bet you didn't know there's flour on the tip of your nose." Before she could blink, he removed it with his thumb. His touch sent an electricity-like spark through her body. "If I don't miss my guess, I would say you've already been hard at work this morning."

She was worried yet excited to show him. "Come in and find out."

Cesare walked through to the kitchen with another bag of food and the empty pan. He put them both on the counter and pulled a phone out of his pocket.

"This is for you. All programmed." He put it at the end of the counter.

Tuccia thanked him, but she had no idea where the batch of tarts he'd left with had ended up. She didn't think she wanted to know.

Without asking her permission, Cesare took a finished product from one of the small round pans. He examined it first. Then he bit into it. An anxious Tuccia waited while he took another bite and another, until it was all gone. *Uh-oh. Here it comes.*

"Why are you closing your eyes?" he asked in a quiet voice.

"I don't know. So I can handle the bad verdict better?"

"On your fourth try, you've achieved perfection. The cinnamon balance is just right. As for the shapes, my mother wouldn't know them from her own. If I didn't have a knowledge of your upbringing, I'd think you came out of the same nunnery." This time he brushed her mouth with his own.

She opened her eyes, trying to contain her joy. "Thank you, Cesare, but you don't have to overdo it."

He ignored her comment. "I'm even more impressed you found something else to cook them in. This apartment is ill-equipped for a chef. When Mamma told me you were resourceful, I don't believe that even she understood the scope of your abilities."

Tuccia scoffed. "She was only quoting my *zia* who thinks I can do no wrong. She and my *zio* wanted babies so much. What they got was me when my parents didn't know what to do with me. Bertina was the one bright light in my existence."

"As you still are in hers," he came back, seemingly deep in thought. "Otherwise she wouldn't have risked everything to help you." His blue gaze swerved to hers, sending more darts of awareness through her body. "That includes using my mother who happens to have the same favorable opinion of you."

"I'll never be able to thank her enough for what she's done. But right this minute I want the honest answer to one question. After talking to your partners, should I be getting ready to leave for Catania?"

He lounged his rock-hard body against the edge of the counter with his arms folded. "I'd like *your* honest answer to another question first. Why did you get up at the crack of dawn and go to all the effort of making another batch when you could have stayed asleep?"

She took a deep breath. "Because I needed to find out for myself if I was capable of following that recipe on my own."

"Which you've demonstrated beyond all doubt. Would it interest you to know my partners devoured the tarts you made?"

"No, they didn't," she said with an embarrassed chuckle.

"One bite told them everything they needed to know. They stuffed themselves and took the few un-eaten mounds with them when they left my room."

"Now you're just trying to make me feel good be-cause…because that's the kind of man you are," she said, her voice faltering.

"You don't have to compliment me back." Yes, she did. She owed him her life right now. "Let me prove it to you."

Tuccia watched him pull out his cell phone and make a call to Vincenzo, the present Duc di Lombardi. They talked for a few moments before he hung up.

"Vincenzo's wife, Gemma, will be arriving within

the hour. Shall we eat the breakfast I brought now? Then I'll clean up the kitchen while you get ready for our guest."

A slight gasp escaped her lips. "Why would she be coming here?"

He reached for the bag of food and set it on the table. "You've passed your first test by baking a dessert the *castello ristorante* would be proud to serve. But this is only the beginning if you decide to accept the daunting challenge facing you."

She averted her eyes. "You're right. It's so daunting, I'm terrified."

"Be frank with Gemma and see what happens."

"What's she like?"

"Only a few years older than you and one of the nicest, kindest women I've ever known."

"Besides being a master pastry chef."

He nodded. "A chef who's about to become a mother. She can't wait for their baby to arrive and is anxious to let someone else take on her former mantle."

"Which no doubt *you* will be doing before the day is out, Cesare. Please forgive me if I skip breakfast. That was very kind of you to bring it, but I'm afraid I can't eat anything right now."

She rushed to the bedroom to take a shower and change into jeans and a knit top. Tuccia had only packed a few understated clothes at Bertina's because she knew she would have to travel light on her trip to Catania and didn't dare stand out.

After being sheltered at Lina Donati's villa for one night, she could never have known she would end up here in Milan to face a situation undreamed of.

Be frank with Gemma.

Tuccia interpreted that to mean she must put the princess part of herself aside. For once she had to dig down to her core and decide if she thought she could pull this off.

This could all end in a second if she asked Cesare to call Vincenzo back and tell him not to bring his wife to the *pensione.* Within a few minutes Tuccia could be driven to the train.

That would leave Cesare to take on the exclusive role of executive pastry chef until he found someone else exceptional, or until Signor Fragala recovered.

But for Tuccia, it would mean never seeing him again. Her heart told her she couldn't handle that. He'd become too important to her.

Sucking in her breath, she reached for the brush to style her curls. Once she'd applied some light makeup and lipstick, she left the bedroom to face what was coming.

Cesare walked outside when he saw Vincenzo's Mercedes pull up in front. While his friend came around from the other side, Cesare helped a blonde, very pregnant Gemma out of the front seat and kissed her cheek. "Thanks for coming."

"It's my privilege. How *à propos* that the princess is staying here in the same apartment I did."

"I thought it the safest place to conceal her."

"You've found the perfect spot tucked out of the way. It takes me back to those first days when I left the *pensione* to meet you for the first time. I was shaking in my boots to be interviewed by the internationally famous restaurateur owner of the Castello Supremo Hotel and Ristorante di Lombardi."

"I would never have known it, Gemma. When you told me your mother's pastry would always be the best, I felt an immediate affinity to you since I felt the same way about my mother's Sicilian cooking. Your desserts were divine."

She kissed his cheek. "Little did I know I would come face to face with Vincenzo when I thought he'd disappeared from my life forever."

Her husband put his arm around her nonexistent waist. "None of us will forget that day. I too thought I'd lost the love of my life. *Grazie a Dio* we found each other."

While his friend chose that moment to kiss Gemma thoroughly, Cesare went back inside the apartment. Tuccia had come in the small living room looking so appealing he'd have liked to do the same thing to her. He was in serious trouble because he knew he couldn't hold back much longer in showing her how he felt.

"They're coming," he said, after answering the question in her misty gray eyes, which were more noticeable because of her black fringed lashes and black hair. She had the most remarkable coloring and light olive complexion. With her oval face and alluring mouth, she looked so irresistible he had to force himself to look away or he'd make her uncomfortable.

He heard the others file inside. "Princess Tuccianna, allow me to present two of my dearest and closest friends, Vincenzo Gagliardi, the Duc di Lombardi, and his wife Gemma."

"It's a real honor for me." Tuccia shook their hands.

"We're the ones honored, Princess," Vincenzo declared. Cesare could tell his friend was bowled over by her beauty, a feat that didn't happen often.

"Please, just call me Tuccia. Won't you sit down? I feel a fraud inviting you into this *pensione* Cesare not only found for me, but is paying for until I can reimburse him."

Cesare noted she was always grace itself. The spoiled princess as reported in the news wasn't the same person he'd pulled against his body a few nights ago for fear she would fall.

"Your desperate situation has called for drastic measures. I had a similar experience in my late teens and was anxious for any help I could get." Leave it to Vincenzo to make her feel comfortable.

"Nevertheless I've put all of you in a dangerous position simply by being here and want you to know I'm ready to leave after we've talked."

Gemma got up from the couch. Cesare noticed that she was a little slower these days. "Tuccia? Before there's any talk like that, why don't you and I go in the kitchen where we can be private and let the guys talk business in here."

Cesare nodded. "That's a good idea." He watched Tuccia follow Gemma into the kitchen. She might be nervous now, but before long she'd realize she couldn't be in better hands than Gemma's. His gaze swerved to his friend.

"How does your wife really feel about this?" he asked in a quiet voice.

"She ate one of the tarts I took back to our room. When she'd finished, she said, 'I know this was Cesare's recipe, but if Tuccia can make all his Sicilian desserts as exquisite as these, the *castello* is going to gain a new following."'

"That's high praise, Vincenzo."

"Gemma is nothing if not truthful."

"If by any chance this works out, I'll insist Tuccia live here and make each dessert in the kitchen first. It will help her feel confident before she leaves for the *castello* every morning to manage her assistants. But I'm afraid that without the right disguise, someone will recognize her and the police will descend."

Vincenzo flashed him a subtle smile. "Meeting her explains a lot. She's a genuine knockout, Cesare. Gemma will be hard-pressed to come up with something that hides her beauty."

"Tell me about it."

"I don't think I have to, *amico*."

No. And the second Takis laid eyes on her, Cesare was in for it. "Was there anything on the morning news I should be concerned about yet?"

"Nothing. The police are at a standstill. Her parents have offered ten million euros for the person who finds her."

"Only ten for their precious daughter?" he bit out in disgust.

"No doubt the *comte*'s reward will be forthcoming before the day is out."

Cesare looked over his shoulder at Tuccia who was deep in conversation with Gemma. "I wonder how much he'd be willing to pay for her safe return. But it won't matter when he gets her letter explaining why she ran away." Cesare confided that he'd couriered it to his attorney in Barbados who would send it on.

"That was excellent thinking."

"She's been suffering terrible guilt."

"Understandable."

"But that part is done. When I arrived here this morning and saw that she'd already been up three hours making the recipe again, I knew for a fact that no amount of money would ever induce her to go back to him."

Vincenzo's brows lifted. "How did she do?"

"Hold on. I'll show you."

Cesare got up and walked into the kitchen. "*Scusa*, ladies." He plucked one of the round pans off the counter and took it into Vincenzo.

His friend reached for an iced tart and ate it in two bites before nodding in satisfaction. "After Gemma and I leave here, we'll drive into Milan and take the rest of these to my cousin and his wife to taste. Dimi will be in shock when we tell him what has happened."

"*Who* will be in shock, *mia cara?*" Gemma had just come back in the living room with Tuccia. Both men stood up.

"I thought we'd visit Dimi before we go back to the *castello* and let them sample Tuccia's nun buns. Did you get your business done?"

"We're off to a good start, aren't we, Tuccia?"

"Your wife has encouraged me to give it a try for which I'm very grateful." The relief on her face was tangible.

"*Meraviglioso!*" Vincenzo picked up the pan and helped his wife out the door to his car. Cesare knew how happy his friend was that someone else was going to be doing the work Gemma had done for so long.

He shut the door and turned to the woman who was transforming his life in ways he couldn't have

imagined days ago. "I'm sure you have a great deal
to discuss with me."

She nodded. "Thankfully Gemma is going to work
two more days while I keep cooking desserts here at
the apartment. Then it'll be my first day in the *castello* kitchen. She'll acquaint me with everything and
stay long enough to introduce me to the staff before
I'm on my own."

"You won't be alone. I'll be there in the background
until you get your bearings. But tell me what it is that
concerns Gemma the most?"

"A disguise for me, especially for my hair."

Her crowning glory was a dead giveaway. "Why
don't you freshen up. Then we'll drive to the uniform
shop in Milan used by the kitchen help. We'll find
something that works. You'll have to wear your scarf
and sunglasses."

"It'll be wonderful to get out for a little while." He
could imagine. "I'll hurry."

After she disappeared, he reached in the fridge for
a soda. Their shopping spree would include a stop to
the grocery store. Once that was done they'd pick up
some takeout and bring it back to the apartment for a
meal. Toward evening they'd get busy working on a
couple of new desserts. He loved being alone with her.

Tuccia hurried out to his sports car. Once again she
had that sensation of being spirited away where nothing could hurt her. But this time she wanted Cesare
to be more than her protector. Though he'd kissed
her several times, she wanted... She wanted the impossible.

He drove them into Milan with expertise and parked

in front of a shop labeled Uniforme di Oggi. "Remember to keep your head mostly down."

"I will."

She couldn't get over the huge selection of chef apparel at the back. While she was taking it all in, Cesare seemed to know exactly what he wanted.

"Here. Try this on."

Cesare handed her a short-sleeved white lab coat that fell above the knee. After she put it on, he shook his head. "It needs to be larger to cover a T-shirt and chef's pants." He handed her a coat two sizes bigger. She tried it on.

"That will do fine. We'll take six of them. Now for six sets of pants and T-shirts that fit. Everything white."

Once she'd pulled the clothes off the racks and handed them to the clerk, they walked over to the counter to look at the chef hats and beanies of all kinds. Again, Cesare already had something in mind and reached for the traditional white floppy hat.

He handed it to Tuccia. "Go in the changing room and try it on where no one will see you. If it's not the right fit, call outside the door to me and I'll get the right one." They walked down the little hall. "Don't get any ideas about slipping out the back way, or you'll be on your own, Principessa." He said it with a slow smile that sent a river of warmth through her body.

Once inside, she removed her scarf and tried on the hat. It was too big. She told him as much. He returned in a minute with a smaller version. This one was just right. It would keep her hair snug inside and prevent any strands from slipping.

She put the scarf and glasses back on before emerging. "This one is the right size."

"Good. We'll take six of them."

He walked her over to the counter and before long they left the shop for his car with her new clothes. Talk about fun. Being with Cesare like this was turning out to be the happiest day of her life. To know the two of them would be working together for months and months was her idea of heaven. She didn't care how hard she had to work.

He drove her around to another store featuring eye glasses. "Stay in the car. I'll be right back."

With his brown hair and tall male physique, he made every man walking along the street look pathetic in comparison. When he came out of the store a few minutes later and flashed her a smile, she couldn't breathe. He handed her a bag with several sets of eye glasses for her to choose from.

"I have an idea," he announced. They'd already left the city for the village. "I'll pick up a meal and ask Takis to join us. My other partner needs to meet you. When he walks in the apartment, I want you to be wearing a complete chef's outfit. Of course he knows what you look like. If you can pass his inspection, then we'll know we have a chance that your identity will remain a secret."

"It *has* to," she whispered.

For a second time in several days Cesare reached for her hand and squeezed it. "This is going to work, Tuccia." She got the feeling he wanted this to work as much as she did. Soon they reached the grocery store and he let go of her. "I'll try not to be too long." He turned on the radio. "In case you want to listen."

While he was gone taking his warmth with him, she moved the tuner and heard the top-of-the-hour news. Her disappearance was still the lead story and a reward was being offered for help in finding her.

How odd that she felt so removed from the princess they were describing. In just a few days she felt like she'd turned into someone else. People were walking around the village and here she was, right in the middle of them with no one the wiser.

Cesare's energy was something to behold. He came back to the car loaded with more groceries and their dinner. She smiled at him. "That was fast. I'm sorry I couldn't be of help." She would adore shopping for groceries with him. Anything where they could be together.

He started the car. "One day all this will be behind you. Let's go home. I gave Takis a call. He'll be here at five which doesn't give you much time to work on your disguise."

"I have an idea about what to do with my hair. If I pull on a nylon stocking first, it will help keep it in place."

"That ought to work. Do we need to buy you some nylons?"

"No. I have a pair with me. Do you think it will be all right if I wear my leather sandals?"

"If they're comfortable, I don't see why not."

When they reached the *pensione*, she got out and helped carry in the bags. "I'll put the clothes in my bedroom."

"Don't come out until you've morphed into a chef. I admit I can't wait to see what you look like."

Neither could Tuccia. After a quick shower she put

on a pair of white semi-baggy drawstring pants. Next came the short-sleeved crew neck T-shirt. Now for the tricky part. She took off the scarf and rummaged in the dresser drawer for a stocking.

She fit it around her head so no hair could escape and pinned it to the crown. After grabbing a chef's hat and sack of eye glasses, she dashed in the bathroom. First she pulled out a pair of the clear lenses with neutral brown frames. Very professional looking. They fit over her ears just fine. Then she put on the hat, slanting the floppy part. The whole thing actually worked. She didn't recognize herself.

Tuccia normally wore a melon colored lipstick. She decided that wouldn't do and wiped off all traces. Pleased with the effect, she went back in the bedroom and pulled on the lab coat. It had pockets and seven buttons down the front opening, leaving the top of the T-shirt exposed. Her figure was non-existent, but that was the whole point.

Still dressed in her sandals, she felt ready for the fashion show. With pounding heart she tiptoed in the living room and found Cesare putting the groceries away. He'd laid the table for their dinner.

"*Signor?* May I have your attention, *per favore*?"

He wheeled around with a sack of flour in his hand. But when he saw her, it dropped to the counter, reminding her of the night in his mother's kitchen. She burst into laughter at the shock on his painfully handsome face.

She moved into the kitchen. "Perhaps you don't recognize me. I'm the new executive pastry chef at the Castello Supremo Hotel Ristorante in Milan, Italy. I can see by your expression that I've achieved a certain amount of success in that department, *signor*."

Loving this, Tuccia turned around like a model on a runway. "If you'll take a closer look, you'll see the detail of the stitching on the pockets of this stunning creation." His eyes played everywhere, as if trying to figure out where she'd gone.

"Pay attention to the large puffy hat, the latest in chic chef wear. This designer was chosen by the world famous five-star restaurateur Cesare Donati. He features nothing but the best in his kitchens, whether here or in New York. It's the greatest privilege I've ever known to be working for him."

His hand rubbed his chest as if he were in a trance. "I saw you go into the bedroom a little while ago," he began in a deep voice. "But I still can't believe it's you underneath all that white."

"Then you think I'll do?"

A knock on the door prevented him from responding. "Come on in, Takis."

Tuccia watched his dark-blond partner walk inside and shut it. Here was another incredibly attractive man who she'd been told had come from the island of Crete. His hazel eyes narrowed on her before he turned to Cesare. "I thought you said that Princess Tuccianna would be here."

"Did you hear that?" Cesare asked her.

"Yes. If the *signori* will excuse me, I'll tell her your guest has arrived for dinner."

She darted back to the bedroom so excited, she had trouble taking off all of her disguise. In a few minutes she returned to the living room with her hair brushed and lipstick on her mouth, wearing the same clothes she'd worn to town with Cesare.

His eyes pierced hers. "Princess Tuccianna, may I present my friend and partner, Takis Manolis."

"I've heard a great deal about you, Signor Manolis. It's a real pleasure to meet you."

He looked taken back. "It *was* you dressed as a chef." A grin broke out on his face. "After knowing what you look like, I would never have guessed. I'm honored to meet you." He shook her hand warmly.

"Even though I'm a wanted fugitive who's putting all of you in jeopardy?"

"Last night Cesare filled us in on the details. After I ate half of those nun buns you made, I told him I believe you'll make an excellent chef. And now that I've seen you in your uniform, I'm convinced no one will recognize you."

"I agree the transformation was miraculous," Cesare murmured. She couldn't wait to hear more about it once they were alone. "Let's eat, shall we? I'm afraid all the shopping we did has worn me out and I'm ravenous."

They sat at the kitchen table where Cesare treated them to scallops, beef *tagliati*, parmesan aubergine and pasta *con le sarde*. Tuccia could hardly believe she was sitting here with these two amazing men, chatting and enjoying the take-out food as if she didn't have a worry in the world. She'd entered into another realm of existence and never wanted to be anywhere else.

"Gemma told me her meeting with you went very well."

"She's a lovely person who answered a lot of questions for me."

"I'll tell you something honestly. She's convinced your Sicilian pastries will create a new sensation with our clientele."

Tuccia put her wine glass down. "You mean Cesare's."

"In time they'll become yours, too."

Takis had a charm almost as lethal as Cesare's. "One dessert does not make a chef, but I'm going to do my very best not to let you down. This evening Cesare will be assigning me a new recipe to cook."

"That's right." Cesare smiled at her. *"Cassateddi."*

She took a deep breath. "Those half-moon-shaped pastries were a favorite of mine growing up, but I never dreamed I'd learn how to make them."

"I loved them, too. So will Takis and Vincenzo. But they're only the beginning. Tomorrow you'll be making *testa di turco*, followed by *sfingi di San Giuseppe, casstelle di Sant'Agata* and Sicilian chocolate torte."

Cesare had just done an excellent job of frightening her to death.

"I think you're overwhelming her, *amico.*"

She leaned toward Takis. "His mother told me he drove her crazy growing up. No matter what she cooked, she'd find some of it missing the second she turned around," Tuccia confided.

Immediately Takis burst into rich male laughter. But Cesare didn't join in.

Too soon their visitor announced that he had to leave and said good-night. She was sorry to see him go because she'd gotten a little carried away with her out-of-school tale where Cesare was concerned. She'd been having too good a time and feared she'd crossed an unmarked boundary in their relationship.

While Cesare walked him out to his car, she hurriedly cleaned up the kitchen. When he came inside, she was already seated at the table with her bible, ready to write down the recipe for what she hoped would turn out to be a worthy *chef d'oeuvre.*

He washed and dried his hands, then he sat down, eyeing her with an intensity that made her squirm. "Tuccia," he began, "I—"

"I know what you're going to say," she broke in on him. "I apologize for saying something so personal in front of your friend. It was wrong of me to overstep like that. I promise it won't happen again."

His brows met in a frown. "I wasn't going to say anything of the sort. Before Takis drove off, he told me you were as sensational as your nun buns and we should keep you at all costs. Takis would never say anything like that unless he meant it."

She looked down because emotion had caused her eyes to smart.

"Before you interrupted me, I was going to tell you the disguise is perfect. I have no doubt you'll be a new trendsetter for the kitchen assistants. They'll take one look at you and want to be just like you, but they'll fail because there's only one Princess Tuccianna."

Tuccia was afraid her cheeks were on fire. She wanted him to forget she was a princess. She wanted him to see her as a woman he could love heart and soul. Looking up she said, "That's absurd, but thank you. Don't you think we should get started on the *cassateddi*? I'll need half the night to make it several times."

Those blue eyes narrowed on her features. "I thought *I* was the slave driver around here."

"Would you rather leave and come back tomorrow morning? I'd understand if you have another engagement."

"I have no plans to meet another woman."

Maybe not tonight. But it didn't mean there wasn't someone who loved him and was waiting anxiously to be with him. She couldn't bear the thought and was ridiculously jealous of any woman he'd been with.

"You're wrong, you know, Tuccia."

"What do you mean?"

"I can read your mind. There's no room in my life for any woman until the *castello*'s new pastry chef can create masterpieces without my help."

Just like that he'd drawn a sharp line in the sand. Meaning she shouldn't get any ideas about him for herself?

She sucked in her breath. "Since I'd hate to see you deprived of that kind of pleasure too long because of me, I'll work day and night to achieve that goal." She tapped the notebook with her pen. "I'm ready when you are."

CHAPTER SIX

Two HOURS LATER Tuccia was in tears. She'd turned out two batches of half-moon shells filled with cream, but they'd been failures. Cesare had tried to eat one and it had fallen apart because she hadn't shaped it right. He had to eat it in pieces. She had to smother a moan watching him.

"The taste of this is superb."

"That doesn't count when its misshape falls apart before reaching your mouth. I tried to execute your directions to the letter, but I couldn't seem to get it right." She dried her eyes with a towel, but they kept falling. "This will never do. I'm going to make the recipe again."

He reached for the towel and wiped her cheeks. "We don't want your tears falling into your next attempt." His comment made her laugh and he kissed both her cheeks before she got started again on a third batch.

His pride in her work ethic kept growing while she took pains to crimp the edges just right. Another hour passed before he tested a sample of her latest work. "I find no fault in this presentation or the taste."

"Thank you," she murmured, but he could tell she still wasn't happy.

Cesare had no doubt that when he left the apartment, she'd make up another batch. Her fighting spirit was a trait he admired more than she would ever know. He stood against the doorjamb and watched while she put the third tray of shells inside the fridge.

"Did Gemma tell you about Maurice Troudeau, our executive chef?"

A corner of her delectable mouth lifted. "She said the key with him was to praise his work often and ask for help once in a while, even if you don't need it. I used that technique on Auguste Senlis, the most difficult history professor at the Sorbonne, and it worked."

Of course it did, but he wasn't smitten because of her smarts. No man anywhere who came into her sphere could remain unaffected. Takis and Vincenzo were a case in point.

"If I have a concern, it's because your French is too perfect. You're a princess on the run who speaks it fluently. Unfortunately you can't afford to speak it with him at all. When I introduce you, you'll be known as Nedda Bottaro from Sicily who speaks Sicilian with a Palermo dialect. Your knowledge of English is too minimal to count on. That's it."

"I understand."

He was sure she did. "Have you thought of a backstory? The staff will ask and you'll have to be ready."

"Yes. I was born in the back room of a bordello in Trapani and never knew my father. My mother didn't, either."

Cesare was having trouble holding back his laughter.

"When I was old enough to be of use, she gave me to the woman next door who was a cook and needed a helper. I never went to school. After my mother died of an infection, I ran away to Palermo and did all kinds of jobs until I prevailed on a baker to let me work for him. I liked that work best and stayed there until I was discovered by you!" Her gray eyes stared straight into his. "What do you think?"

At this minute he didn't dare tell her what he thought or felt. He was in love with her. "I have one suggestion. At least say that you went to school once in a while. Your intelligence shines through in everything you say and do."

"So does yours. Thank you for tonight's cooking lesson. I'll see you in the morning."

If she had any idea he would rather stay with her all night and every night, she'd fly out the door. "Tuccia? Before I leave, let's go in the living room and talk for a minute about something serious. You've been cooped up here for several days, no doubt missing a few friends to talk to."

Cesare went in the other room first so she'd follow. They both sat down. He took a chair and she the couch. "I know you've run away from your parents, but deep down this has to be torturous for you."

She curled up against the side. "If I told you the truth, I'm afraid you might think me a person with no natural affection."

He steadied himself. "Explain that."

"I know you're supposed to love your parents. I suppose I do in a philosophical way, but it's Zia Bertina I've always turned to. She was the mother I needed. My own was cold and my father was always a stranger to me. When I think of them, I get an empty feeling inside. With a mother like yours, I know you can't comprehend it."

Cesare shifted in the chair. "You're right." He had no words.

"I don't tell you this so you'll feel sorry for me, but only to explain that I've lived with this situation for twenty-five years. Your concern for my feelings has touched me very much, but you needn't worry yourself on my account because I have to stay secluded. As long as I have my *zia* who has loved me all my life, I'm happy."

He sucked in his breath. "But it's still not too late for you to leave Milan and do what you want, whether in Catania or elsewhere. You should be able to embark on a new life, work at something that interests you and make new friends."

"Find a lover *I've* chosen?" she added in a voice that made her sound much older.

He closed his eyes for a moment. "Why not?"

"I never wanted the fiancé I can't stand, let alone some lover, followed by another and then another that goes on and on like a revolving door. We royals are known for it. To be honest I can't think of anything worse."

Neither could Cesare.

"Right now there's just one thing on my mind. To prove that I can make a success of something truly important, not only to me, but to you and your partners. Your *ristorante* is without a pastry chef. If I could pull this off, nothing would make me happier."

Her earnestness crept through him, causing his throat to swell. "I believe you mean that."

She nodded. "I've surprised myself. Do you know what a shock it is to discover that I *like* such pains-taking work? Who would have thought I'd find it a challenge to crimp the edges of those half moons so they were just right? But if you think there's still too much danger, or that it's really not going to work, then please tell me now and I'll leave whenever you say."

Humbled by an inner purity in her, Cesare got up from the chair. When he'd suggested they come in the living room for a little talk, he never expected to feel his heart torn apart by the confessions of a girl whose parents hadn't been able to show her how precious she was.

The backstory she'd concocted for the staff could only have come from a princess who'd been born with every advantage under the sun except love.

"Rest assured we need you right here, Tuccia." He leaned over to kiss her lips briefly, unable to help himself. But if she'd wanted to respond, he didn't give her the chance and stood up. "Stay where you are. You look too comfortable to move. I'll let myself out and see you in the morning with breakfast and more groceries."

After a detour to the kitchen for one of the pans of *cassateddi* to share with his friends, he left for the *castello* a different man than the one he'd been four hours ago.

On the drive home, Cesare pulled out his cell to call his mother. He was glad to hear that his sister was there visiting with her husband and baby. They all chatted for a few minutes until Isabella got off the line.

"Now we can talk about important matters, Cesare. I have to tell you Bertina is out of her mind with worry."

"Let her know I just came from being with Tuccia. She sends her love and wants to assure her *zia* all is well. She would phone, but knows the police have tapped the lines."

"I'm sure of it. Tuccia is really all right?"

"Would I tell you otherwise?"

"No, *figlio mio*. I trust you with my life."

"That's nice to hear. Does Bertina have any more news about the search?"

"The police are baffled. Their bungling has enraged her sister and brother-in-law. Bertina's sources tell her that Jean-Michel is so overcome he has remained incommunicado to the media. There's been no ransom note and they fear for her welfare."

"I have something to tell you, Mamma." In the next breath he told her about the letter being sent to Jean-Michel. "Once he receives it, everything will change."

"It can't get to him soon enough!"

"I agree." In the meantime Tuccia would hear the worst when she turned on her TV. "I hope Bertina is putting on the show of her life to prove how grief-stricken she is."

"If I didn't know the truth, I'd be convinced she's in the depths of despair. I've decided she could have been a great actress."

Superb acting appeared to run in the royal family. Tuccia's fashion show earlier this evening had stunned him close to speechless.

"One more thing you should know, Cesare. Bertina says Tuccia's parents are truly distraught over the situation and she can tell this experience has caused them to realize it's their fault that she's run away. They are beside themselves with worry and she senses a softening."

"That's wonderful news, Mamma." When he could, he'd relay that message to Tuccia. "Tell me about Ciro."

"If there are no more complications, he'll be taken to a private room tomorrow."

"We'll hope for the best. I have to hang up now, but I'll call you soon. *Bona notti*, Mamma."

It was ten after one in the afternoon and Tuccia still hadn't finished cooking this latest recipe. She let out a moan. "These *sfingi di San Giuseppe* balls are all wobbly. I can't make them even."

Cesare chuckled. Nothing seemed to bother him. The man had arrived early that morning in jeans and a silky claret-colored open-necked sport shirt looking devilishly gorgeous. There ought to be a law against it.

She hadn't slept all night remembering the taste of his mouth on hers. He wouldn't have kissed her if he didn't have feelings for her. It was the reason she'd been a mess after he'd left the apartment the night before. Since then she'd been reliving that moment and wanted to repeat the experience. But this time she wouldn't let him go.

"They're supposed to look like that."

"No, they're not! What am I doing wrong?"

"Nothing. When they're fried, their centers will hollow out so you can fill them."

She shot him a glance. "You promise?"

"I swear it. Have you put out the toweling?"

"It's right here on the counter next to the stove."

"Have you checked the temperature of the olive oil?"

"Yes. The thermometer says it's ready."

"Then get started. Remember not to let the ball plop, but don't be afraid of it."

Tuccia began the laborious process of cooking and draining. They smelled good and everything was going fine until the last one. It fell off the spoon too fast and some drops of oil splashed on her wrist. She cried out in surprise.

Cesare was there so fast he had her hand under the cold water before she could think. "Keep it there for a few minutes," he said while he removed the oil and turned off the burner.

"I tried to be careful, but I was clumsy."

"I defy anyone cooking with oil for the first time to escape with no burns."

While the water was still running he examined the three small welts on her skin. "These will hurt, but I have a remedy my mother used that works well."

She couldn't feel the pain, not while their bodies were so close and he was touching her. "Thank you," she said in a tremulous voice before lifting her head.

His eyes searched hers before his free hand caressed the side of her face. "I'm sorry you got burned," he whispered.

Tuccia felt his breath on her lips. Her heart felt like it was going to pump right out of her chest. Driven by her love for him, she pressed her mouth to his, daring to let him know she wanted more. "It's nothing," she whispered, then quickly turned to put her hand under the water once more.

He moved away from her. "I'll run to the *farmacia* and be right back." Cesare was out the door before she could think. It was just as well. If he'd stayed close to her a second longer, she would have made a complete fool of herself and thrown her arms around his neck.

She'd never known the white-hot heat of desire for a man until now. To experience its power for herself was life-changing. The few guys at college she'd flirted with in class had meant nothing more than a little experimentation that couldn't go anywhere.

Though she'd always planned to run away before she had to marry Jean-Michel, she never expected to find loving fulfillment with one man. Tuccia hadn't believed such a thing was possible. First she had to *find* the right man, and he had to find *her*.

But when she heard the door open and Cesare walked back in the apartment with a small sack in his hand, she knew beyond a shadow of a doubt she was looking at the right man. The *only* man for her. She felt it in the marrow of her bones.

Tuccia turned off the water and waited. He walked over to the counter and pulled from a shelf the bottle of honey she'd used in one of the recipes. Next, he opened the sack and drew out some gauze pads and a small box of plasters.

Without looking at her he covered the gauze with honey and said, "Put out your arm and we'll get rid of that pain."

Tuccia did his bidding. Within a minute he'd covered the three welts with the gooey gauze pads and secured them with a plaster. She marveled at his dexterity. "I had no idea honey could be used like this."

"It has dozens of restorative elements."

"Thank you, Cesare. I'm very lucky to have a boss who's a doctor, too."

He smiled a smile that sent her pulse off the charts. "You should be feeling relief soon."

"That's good because I need to poke a hole in those balls and fill them with the ricotta cream I've made."

Cesare darted her a glance. "All of it will keep. Before you do any more cooking, I thought we'd pick up lunch and have a picnic. It will give those burns a chance to settle down."

"A picnic? I'd love it! When I think about it, I haven't been on one of those since I was a little girl. My *zia* would take me to the park and we'd feed the birds. I'll grab the things I need and meet you at the car."

She dashed into the bedroom for her scarf. When she'd put it on, she slid her sunglasses in place and hurried out of the apartment. Cesare, the striking, quintessential Sicilian male, was there to help her in and they drove off.

For once in her life, what was happening to her wasn't a dream her mind had concocted while she'd been asleep. She was wide awake. This was real. Her feelings were real and she wanted to shout to the world that she was madly in love with him.

He stopped at a local deli for takeout and they headed toward Milan. Before long he turned onto the grounds of the Giardino Della Guastalla. "These gardens are five hundred years old," he explained. "I know the perfect spot where we can be alone. Maybe we'll be able to feed a few birds the remnants of our lunch. Do you mind sitting on the grass?"

"To be out in nature is exactly what this warm day calls for."

He parked and they walked to a lush spot beneath a giant oak tree. The freedom to be out here alone with Cesare made her giddy. After removing her sunglasses, she lay down in the grass on her stomach and rested her head against her arms.

"Careful of those burns," he said, sitting down next to her.

She squinted up at him. "Honestly? I forgot I was hurting. Your honey has worked miracles."

"I'm glad." Cesare opened up the cartons. She turned on her side and leaned on one elbow while they ate shrimps and pasta salad with little forks. He opened a bottle of red wine and poured it into cups. She drank some and munched on a French bread roll.

"I feel sinful lying here."

Blue eyes full of amusement roved over her. "Because you're with me instead of your former fiancé?"

"No." She smiled. "Because I'm with someone I care about to the exclusion of anyone else," she said before it was too late to stop her thoughts from becoming verbal.

He drank the rest of his wine. "Surely there've been some men you've liked who have tried to have a secret relationship with you?"

"I was always under surveillance, Cesare." She looked at him through veiled eyes. "As you know, there are different levels of liking without much emotional involvement. I liked some of the guys in my classes, but didn't have the freedom to do anything about it. But to actually care for someone means having the time to explore feelings that touch on the deeper elements of the human heart."

Realizing she'd said too much, Tuccia sat up and wound her arms around her upraised knees. "I'm afraid I've embarrassed you when I didn't mean to."

Cesare leaned closer. "Why would I be embarrassed to be paid a compliment like that?"

She put her sunglasses back on. "You always know the right thing to say, so I'll never see what's really going on inside you. But I'm thankful for this moment out of time to enjoy the company of a man revered by his mother and his friends. No men from my world can claim that distinction."

"Do you mind if I ask you a question about Jean-Michel?"

"Of course not."

"When your marriage was arranged, had you already met him?"

"No. My parents gave one of their many parties at our palazzo and insisted I attend. I was only sixteen and had refused to go because I couldn't bear to be around grownups. But this time my father came to my room carrying a long dress. He said he would wait while I put it on. It was humiliating to be walked from my apartment to the grand ballroom like I was a baby.

"He led me through their usual set of guests to my mother. She was standing next to a man twice my age I didn't recognize and didn't like on sight. He was shorter than my father and overdressed, reminding me of a peacock. I shrank from his dark eyes where the lids remain at half mast like some French men's.

"My father introduced me to Jean-Michel Ardois, the son of Comte Ardois of Paris. He wasn't Sicilian, another huge strike against him. The man kissed my hand and slid a ring with a crest on my finger. While I stood there in shock, my father announced our engagement."

Tuccia smiled at the man who'd become the center of her universe. "Aren't you sorry you asked?"

His expression had sobered. "I want to know everything about you. Where's the betrothal ring now?"

"I'm sure it has been returned to Jean-Michel. I left it on the floor of the ladies' room at the salon."

He studied her features. "How often did you have to spend time with him?"

"Twice a year I endured a visit from him at my parents' palazzo until my father enrolled me at the University of Paris. He said I would have to learn French in order to be the *comte*'s wife. Once my parents took an apartment there, I had to go to the ballet or the opera with him every few months. Several times we went horseback riding on the Ardois estate. Our desultory conversations were worse than waiting for a train that never seems to come."

Cesare drank more wine. "You're not only articulate, you paint haunting pictures. Tell me more."

It was wonderful being able to open her thoughts and heart to him. "The first time we went out alone, I made up my mind I would run away before the marriage on my twenty-fifth birthday. If I could have disappeared the night of the betrothal, I would have. But I was never left alone until that morning at the salon for my dress fitting,"

"Literally never?" He sounded incredulous.

"Never. My parents accused me of being a willful child and didn't trust me. Someone was always watching me, even when I stayed with Zia Bertina."

A strange sound came out of him. "Did he ever try to take advantage of you?"

"Yes. I was so disgusted I slapped his face hard and pushed him off me. It left a red mark that probably branded him for several hours."

"Did he try to accost you every time you were together?"

She could tell Cesare's dislike for Jean-Michel was growing more intense. "No. I don't think he dared for fear I'd do something worse. Instead he bided his time until he had legal power over me. *Grazie a Dio* that never happened."

On that note she got to her feet and put the cartons back in the bag with the rest of the wine. To her surprise he stood up and put his arms around her from behind. "I thank God it didn't happen to you, either." He kissed her neck.

Tuccia could have died of happiness right there, but a group of people were walking by. Cesare had seen them, too, because he let go of her.

"We—we need to get going so I can finish the *sfingi* and start the *testa di turco*," she stammered. Before he could say anything else she added, "My arm is so much better I can hardly believe it, so you don't have to worry that I can't work anymore today, Dr. Donati."

His quiet laughter hid whatever he was really thinking. Together they walked to the car. He gave her arm a squeeze before helping her get in. She'd wanted him to crush her against him and tell her he was in love with her, too.

Unfortunately this interlude was over, but it was yet another one with him she'd always treasure. The memories were stacking up and her love for him was exploding.

CHAPTER SEVEN

WHEN THE LAST batch of *testa di turcos* were finished and decorated, Cesare proclaimed them perfect and announced he was leaving. One more day tomorrow to guide Tuccia through two more recipes and then this private time with her was over.

He would no longer have a legitimate reason to come to the *pensione*. From that point on their business would have to be conducted at the *castello* kitchen. A limo could take her back and forth. After today he realized he couldn't afford to be in such close quarters with her. Her burns had given him a reason to touch her, something he should never have done.

To see her lying there in the grass while he wanted to get down there with her and kiss them into oblivion had almost killed him. Another time like that and he'd have to act on his desire. If those people hadn't walked by while he was kissing her neck, he would have pulled her back down and shown her how he felt.

But he'd picked up enough on hearing her talk about her life with her parents to realize how lonely, how empty her life had been. Being forced to think about marriage at the age of sixteen *was* criminal, as his mother had said. Cesare refused to be the man who came along at the most vulnerable time in her life and took away her chance to be emotionally free.

Today at the park he *knew* she wanted him. But she deserved marriage. That was the only way Cesare would make love to her. She would have to be his legal wife, but the situation with Jean-Michel wasn't yet resolved. And deep down inside, he didn't feel worthy of her.

"Cesare?" His head jerked around. "I guess you didn't hear me. Who is the person who prints the menus for the guests? How far ahead do I have to get the names of the desserts to that person?"

"Don't worry about that yet. Gemma's pastries will be served until next Monday." He was impressed she'd been thinking that far ahead.

Tuccia bit her lip. "What about the ingredients that come to the kitchen from town? Am I in charge of ordering them, or do I coordinate with Maurice? There's so much I don't know."

"How could you have learned everything in a few days?" Her ability to consider all the ramifications of her new job astounded him. "I'll be there to answer your questions.

"Right now we're concentrating on your feeling good about the half-dozen desserts you're mastering. That way you'll have confidence talking to your assistants and giving them instructions on how to prepare what you've planned. I promise things will fall into place. Now I have to leave."

She walked him to the door. "I can't tell you how nice it was to eat at the park this afternoon. If you're tired of my thanking you, then you'll just have to get used to it."

"That works both ways. You're helping me so I don't have to go back to doing a chef's job I gave up a long time ago. We're even."

Tuccia shook her head. "No, we're not." She clung to the open door. "How long were you a chef?"

"From the moment I arrived in New York. The pay put me through part of college. I took out a loan to buy a small restaurant that was going under and called it Mamma's. People love Sicilian food and pretty soon I'd made enough money to buy another restaurant."

She let out a sigh. "And history was made. It explains why you're such an expert teacher. Your mother must have been so proud of you to leave Sicily and put your stamp on the world. *I'm* proud of you, Cesare. Does your father have any idea what an outstanding son he has?"

No one had ever asked him that. Her sweetness was getting to him. He rubbed the back of his neck. "I don't even know if he's alive. When he left my mother, she never saw or heard from him again."

"What a tragedy for him. Your father missed out on the whole point of life. I'd love to meet him and tell him what a fantastic son he has."

Cesare cleared his throat. "I thought the same thing about your parents when you told me about your emptiness."

A shadow crossed over her stunning features. "Forget me."

That would be impossible.

Donati. If you stay here talking to her any longer, you're a fool.

"I spoke with my mother earlier. She said your parents are genuinely upset over your disappearance. I was glad to hear it. Bertina sees a fissure in the ice where they are concerned. I just thought you should know."

Her eyes clouded over. "That's pretty hard to believe."

"I don't think she would have said anything if she didn't think it were true." He kissed her temple. "See you in the morning. I'll make breakfast when I get here. Same time?"

She nodded, causing her black curls to shimmer. He longed to plunge his fingers into that silky mass and devour her.

Without lingering any longer, he walked out to the car and drove away without looking back. Needing a distraction, he turned on the radio and found a twenty-four-hour news station. But he didn't hear anything about her case until he'd pulled into the parking area of his favorite sports bar in the village.

That's when he learned that Interpol was now involved to coordinate police cooperation throughout Europe in order to find the princess.

After shutting off the engine, he went inside and ordered, a pale lager from a Lombardi brewery both he and Takis enjoyed. While he waited for the waiter to bring some appetizers, he phoned Vincenzo. His friend wouldn't be taking Gemma to their home in Lake Como until next week. Cesare needed some advice and no one had a better head.

He reached Vincenzo's voice mail and asked him to call him when he could. Once he'd finished his lager, he headed for the *castello* and let himself in his private office off the lobby. While he did some work on the computer that had been piling up, his friend returned the call and Cesare talked to him about Tuccia's disappearance.

"Tonight I heard that Interpol is now involved. It's getting ugly. Tuccia has sent Jean-Michel a letter of apology. He should be getting it soon. But part of me wants to urge her to get in touch with him right away and settle this thing quietly with him and her parents. The press could then be informed that she's safe and they've called off their marriage."

A long silence ensued. "In a perfect world, Cesare. But I was born in her *imperfect* one. She's done something uncommonly courageous. It's just my opinion, but I think she needs to see it through on her own inspiration, come what may. That's what *I* did with no regrets."

It was the "come what may" part that made Cesare shudder. He couldn't ignore what she'd told him at the park about her caged life, but he valued Vincenzo's judgment. "Thanks for listening. I appreciate it."

"We've been through a lot together, *amico*. Are you going to be all right?"

"I'll have to be, won't I."

He hung up. There'd be little sleep for him tonight. Instead of going up to his room, he began printing off copies of the recipes she'd been following under his supervision. When the time came, she would have to hand them to her assistants.

Dozens of other tasks needed to be taken care of. Why not now while adrenaline surged through his veins over the cruelty Tuccia had endured this far in her life. She'd been robbed of a normal existence. If he didn't have responsibilities, he'd disappear with her to some hidden spot on the other side of the globe and love her without worrying about anything else.

This morning Tuccia had got up at five-thirty to finish her surprise for Cesare and make some rolls. She'd started their breakfast before she'd gone to bed and hoped he'd love it. He'd done so much for her that she wanted to do this small thing to repay him. Today would be their last for working together alone.

In the past when she'd gone out on the royal yacht with her parents and their friends in the summer, one of the aspects she looked forward to was the Sicilian breakfast served on board. Curious to know how *granita* was made, she'd prevailed on the cook to show her.

When the mixture of sugar, water and almond paste was melted, then frozen, stirred, mashed, frozen, stirred, mashed and frozen many times until it came out looking like snow, it was served in a goblet. Eaten with a yeast brioche, it tasted like heaven. The cook also made fruit *granitas* topped with whipping cream, but she'd preferred the almond and dipped her roll in it.

From the window over the sink she saw Cesare arrive. It was ten to eight. He was early! Every time he came to the apartment, excitement exploded inside her. Thank goodness she'd set the table ahead of time and had made coffee. She'd even designed a menu for him, describing what he would be eating. She folded and propped it where his plate would go.

Though she wanted to fling the door open and run into his arms, she steeled herself to wait until he knocked before answering the door. The second he walked in wearing a dark blue polo shirt and white trousers, he paused. His gaze zeroed in on her.

"Something smells wonderful."

Somebody *looked* wonderful.

"I'm glad. Welcome to Tuccia's, Signor Donati!" She made a sweep with the arm that had fresh honey gauze pads taped over her burns. They wouldn't be necessary after today. "If you'll come in and find a seat, I'll be your server."

She watched him walk in the kitchen and sit down to examine the menu. His head reared. He stared at her with a stunned expression. *"Granita di mandorle?"*

"Si, signor."

Delighted with his reaction, she rushed to pour their coffee. She'd already put sugar on the table because he liked a lot of it. Then she pulled two filled snifters out of the small freezer compartment. After putting them on a plate with a warm roll, she set them on the table and sat down.

Tuccia had already tasted it and knew it was good. Not as good as the cook on the yacht had made it, but she was proud of it. Out of the corner of her eye she watched Cesare take his first few bites, wishing he were her husband so they could do this every morning.

Pretty soon he was dipping his roll into the concoction the way she always did. Halfway through his meal, he ran out of roll and reached for her hand across the table.

"You told me you didn't know how to cook anything except to make instant coffee and tea in the microwave."

"I forgot about this. I love it so much I begged the cook on my parents' yacht to teach me how."

He released her fingers. "It's superb...just the right taste and consistency. You must have been up all night."

"I wanted to treat *you* for a change. It was worth it."

He seemed taken back. "My mother's version isn't as good as this one. We're going to be serving your rendition for one of our nightly desserts starting next week."

She moaned. "It's so much work!"

His deep laughter filled the kitchen. "That's what the assistants are for. I have a gut feeling our fame for fine Sicilian cuisine is going to spread and we'll be inundated with too many would-be guests to accommodate."

He got up from the table and brought back a plate with more rolls. Having finished off the flavored ice, he devoured the rest of them in no time at all. "These are delicious by the way. You're such a fast learner it's breathtaking. I'm convinced you could do anything at all if you put your mind to it."

"I think you're flattering me into giving you another serving of *granita.* I made enough if you want more now."

"I'll definitely want some later." He sat back in the chair. "Tell me. Would you rather lie down for the rest of the morning and catch up on some much-needed sleep? Later on this afternoon I'll come back and we'll work on the chocolate torte. Once you've made it, we won't have to worry about your cooking anything new for a few days."

"I'd rather do it now if you don't mind. Then I'll be able to relax enough to face tomorrow."

"So be it. Let's get started. I'll clear the table while you find your bible."

"It's on the shelf." She got up to reach for it and saw Cesare put the menu in his trouser pocket. If that meant what she hoped it meant, all the hard work and loss of sleep had been worth it.

Later, while she was icing her next five-layer creation, Cesare's cell phone rang. She kept working while he walked in the living room. He didn't come back to the kitchen for at least fifteen minutes. She couldn't read his expression.

"Is everything all right?"

He lounged against the wall with his hands in his pockets. "Ciro took a turn for the worse during the night and has ended back up in the ICU."

"His heart?"

"Yes."

"How sad." She waited to hear more. "What else is wrong? I know it's something serious."

"I'd rather not have to tell you this, but you have the right to know."

"What is it?" Her voice shook.

"My mother had just arrived at Bertina's palazzo to prepare meals this morning when the police showed up without notice and took her to police headquarters for further questioning."

Tuccia put a hand to her mouth.

"Mamma returned to the villa to phone me. The police know that Bertina is the person you've always turned to and that she was the one who chartered the jet for you. Naturally they believe she knows where you are hiding."

"Of course."

"Just remember your aunt is a strong woman who loves you very much. She says your parents have softened a great deal and went to the station with her to lend their support."

"You're kidding—"

"No. I really do think they are suffering over what they did to you. Mamma and I agree she'll be able to handle an interrogation. The police don't have evidence of any kind. Bertina doesn't know where you are, only that you're safe. The police won't be able to hold her."

"The situation is growing unbearable. I could end all the pain for Bertina by just going home."

In the next breath Cesare walked over and put his hands on her shoulders. He looked into her eyes. "That's not going to be necessary. Once Jean-Michel gets your letter, he'll tell the police and the princess hunt will be over. But if you feel strongly about this, I'll fly you to Palermo today to see your aunt."

"I know you would, but I couldn't let you down now."

"Forget about me."

"You're too wonderful to be real." She buried her face in her hands. "I wish I knew what to do. I don't want my *zia* to suffer, but I've made a commitment to you. Hearing the bad news about Ciro only makes things worse."

Cesare pulled her against him and wrapped his arms around her. "I have an idea that will make the most sense. Let's wait another day until I hear from my mother. Hopefully your fiancé will have gotten your letter. Nothing may be as bad as you're imagining."

His tenderness was too much. Tuccia broke down sobbing quietly against his chest, unable to stop. "Forgive me for soaking your shirt. I'm a disaster and you shouldn't have to put up with me for another second."

"What if I want to."

When she tried to pull away, he lowered his head and started kissing her wet face until his mouth covered hers. It all happened so naturally that her lips opened. In another second she experienced the full intensity of a kiss that thrilled her to the very depths of her being.

"Cesare—" she cried, so completely besotted she started kissing him back with a passion she didn't know herself capable of. For this fabulous man to be loving her like this brought a rush of joy to her heart she could hardly contain.

"Forgive me if I've been needing this," he whispered in a shaken voice. "You have no idea how you've affected me. Tuccia—" He drew her so close there was no air between them. "Tell me to stop."

"I can't. I want you to go on kissing me and never stop." Once again they were devouring each other. The more she clung to him, the more she realized she'd never be able to appease this growing hunger for him. He'd come into her life and changed it forever.

She wanted him with her whole heart and soul, but if he was only kissing her in order to comfort her, then she had to do something to turn this around. All he needed now was to have to worry about being stuck with a fugitive who was desperate for love and attention and had begged him to let her remain here and work for him.

It was up to her to see this for what it was and not get carried away. Deep down she was fearful he saw her in that light. How could he not? She broke their kiss and wheeled out of his arms. It took all her strength to turn and face him head-on, knowing her cheeks were flushed and her lips swollen.

Tuccia had to prove that he could count on her. "I—I'm afraid we both got carried away," she stammered. "You're a very attractive man. I'm shocked you're not married yet. Any woman could lose her head with you. I'm no exception. I've thought about what you said. It would be best to give the situation another twenty-four hours before I make any kind of decision that could impact both of us."

"I was hoping you'd say that."

She could believe it. The man was depending on her to keep her head at this point. Needing to stay busy, she cut a piece of torte and handed it to him on a plate with a fork. "Try this and tell me what you think."

Please just do it, Cesare.

He did her bidding, eating half of it before putting the plate on the table. "You pass with flying colors, Tuccia."

"It was your recipe." Relief swamped her. "You don't think I need to make it again right now to improve it?"

"No." His eyes had narrowed on her mouth. Her heart felt like it was running away with her. "The torte is exquisite."

"Then do you mind if I lie down for a little while?"

One brow lifted. "I was about to suggest it. You need sleep. I'll come by at five with a meal and we'll talk over what's going to happen tomorrow."

"Thank you for understanding." She took a quick breath. "Thank you for everything."

"Try not to worry too much, Tuccia."

"That would be impossible."

He looked like he was going to say something, then thought the better of it. The moment he walked out of the apartment, she locked the door, then ran to the bedroom and flung herself on the bed in agony. After fleeing from a man she'd despised, she'd run straight into a man she adored.

Tuccia wondered if she dared tell him exactly what she felt, that she loved him and wanted to be his wife. Maybe that was what she would do the next time they were together. No more holding back.

At ten to five, Cesare, showered, shaved, and wearing a tan summer suit, walked in the *castello* kitchen. He nodded to Maurice before packing a bag of *fettuccini Alfredo* with chicken to go. Nothing else was needed. Tuccia had cooked rolls and cake that morning. There was still a half bottle of Chardonnay waiting to be enjoyed with another snifter of her fabulous *granita.*

Princess Tuccianna was so full of surprises he decided there wasn't anything she couldn't do. One taste of her mouth and he knew he wanted to go on tasting it for the rest of his life. When she'd surrendered herself to him, he'd experienced ecstasy like nothing he'd ever known and had come close to having a heart attack.

He'd sensed he was in deep water the first night he'd caught her in his arms in his mother's kitchen. But since then his feelings for her had escalated to such a degree his life had been irrevocably changed.

She was in his heart, in his blood, but that wasn't enough. Cesare wanted her in his life day and night. He wanted her in his bed. He wanted babies with her.

He wanted everything that he'd feared would never happen because he hadn't believed love would come to him.

Yet now that he'd found this extraordinary woman, he feared it was too soon to tie her down with his own needs. For years her parents had exerted too much pressure on her to conform to their demands, and she'd run away.

After the ecstasy of their kiss, Cesare wanted to marry her and never let her go. But Cesare sensed that would be the wrong thing to do. She needed time to develop her sense of self first.

The greatest gift he could give her would be to hold back and allow her to become the incredible person he knew her to be. As long as she worked for him, he could keep her close to him until the time came when he had to tell her how he felt.

On his way out of the kitchen he walked over to Gemma who was setting up for the evening crowd. It was a good thing tonight would be her last night as pastry cook. Her baby would be coming before long. She needed rest.

"Tuccia and I will be here at nine in the morning."

"I'll be watching for you. Is she nervous?"

"She doesn't show it."

Gemma smiled at him. "What about you, Cesare?"

"I know she's going to be fine."

"With you helping her, she couldn't possibly go wrong."

If Gemma had seen him kissing Tuccia earlier as if his life depended on it—which it did—she would probably have told him to slow down. He kissed Gemma's cheek and left the *castello* for his car.

On the way down to the village he turned on the five o'clock news. Following the latest world events he learned there'd been a break in the case involving Princess Tuccianna's disappearance. But the police weren't revealing the details yet. That had to mean the letter had reached Jean-Michel.

Pleased by the new development, he turned it off and pulled up in front of the *pensione*. Tuccia must have seen him arrive because she opened the door for him, appearing to have gotten some rest.

This evening she wore the same print blouse and pants from a few nights ago. Her wardrobe didn't consist of more than three or four changes of clothes. The apartment's washer and dryer had been a necessity, but he intended to rectify the situation and take her shopping.

She eyed the bag he carried. "More goodies?"

"Maurice's version of *fettuccini*."

"I can't wait to try it. Then I can compliment him on it tomorrow. Come in." Tuccia closed the door and followed him into the kitchen. She'd cleaned it spotless and had set the table. The TV was on in the living room. "I've been listening to the news."

"So have I," he stated and reached for some plates to serve their dinner. "We both know what that new development in your case means. By now Jean-Michel will have called off the search. Within the next few hours he'll make some kind of statement to the press. In the meantime I'm sure your aunt is going to be fine, otherwise I would have heard from my mother by now."

"I pray you're right."

"Even so, the letter provides proof that you're alive.

Therefore your family will have to hire private detectives to look for you if they are still intent on finding you. According to Bertina, they're hoping you'll come home because they love you. So I'd say tonight is a time for celebration!"

He reached for the Chardonnay and poured it into glasses before putting them on the table. "Where are your delicious rolls?"

"There were four left. I put them in the microwave and will warm them up."

When they finally sat down at the table, he raised his wine glass. "Before we eat, I'd like to make a toast." Her gray eyes sparkled as she lifted hers. "To the princess who overnight has turned into a pastry cook *par excellence.*"

"I'm going to try." They touched glasses and sipped their wine. "Now I'd like to make one." She raised her glass again, staring straight into his eyes. "To her teacher, a man who is without equal."

Cesare wished it were true.

Everything she said and did had such impact he didn't know where to go with his feelings without betraying them. But he'd made himself a promise to keep things professional for a while longer. She, too, was behaving as if their soul-destroying kiss that morning had changed nothing.

But they both knew that it had.

All he could do was clink her glass and drink more wine.

"Hmm," she said after tasting the *fettuccini.* "This is exceptional. I can see why Maurice was hired."

"We've been very happy with him." Cesare ate another of her rolls. "It's a balmy night out. After we finish dinner, would you like to go for a drive while we talk about tomorrow?"

"You must be reading my mind. I was afraid to ask."

She'd probably be shocked if she knew what was going through his. He'd rather take her in the other room and dance with her. Unfortunately if he did that, they would end up in the bedroom and not come back out for days. So much for him following his own advice to put those thoughts out of his mind.

He took a deep breath. "I thought I'd show you around the *castello* estate to get you acquainted. You'll enjoy seeing the swans on the lake."

"Ooh. How beautiful."

"It's quite a sight on a moonlit night, though the moon won't be out for several hours. When we return, I'll finish off the *granita* and another slice of torte."

After they finished eating and had cleared the table, they walked outside and took off in the car. Tuccia turned to him in her seat. "I've wanted to see the fortress up close. It has such a rich history. I can hardly believe that Vincenzo's family home has been turned into a hotel and restaurant."

"Vincenzo's father and uncle squandered everything and the estate was seized by the government to be sold to the highest bidder. Vincenzo asked me and Takis if we wanted to pool our assets and buy it with him."

"When was this?"

"The three of us were in New York at the time. He had the idea to turn it into the business proposition it is today. That way he could preserve his family legacy and do something honorable for the region. I thought it a fantastic idea. So did Takis."

"Bravo for Vincenzo," she exclaimed. "I can understand that happening in a family as power-hungry as his. It's the only reason my parents made sure early in my life that they would have a son-in-law with a fortune. That would be their insurance to keep them living their lavish lifestyle to the end of their days."

Her words caused Cesare's stomach muscles to clench. He drove them to the summit and took the road that wound behind the *castello*.

"This place is massive."

"You're right."

Two sets of guests from the hotel were out walking. He drove the car past them until they reached the lake much further away. She rolled down her window. "It's so lovely and peaceful, but I don't see any swans."

"They're probably hiding in the rushes, but they'll come out." Cesare turned off the engine and turned toward her. "Tomorrow will be here before you know it. Gemma is ready to ease many of your concerns. But I'd like to know what is worrying you most and relieve you if I can."

Tuccia shook her head. "Do you know what I wish? That I could have been a normal person you'd hired at one of your restaurants in New York. Think how much I could have learned from you."

He had news for her. If she'd come into his life back then, they'd be married by now. He wouldn't have hesitated asking her. "Instead you're learning to be a pastry chef here."

"But it isn't fair to you," her voice cracked.

"Tuccia…"

"It's true. You're playing a dangerous game in order to protect me, Cesare. I honestly don't know what Jean-Michel would do if he caught up to you."

Cesare smiled. "I'm afraid you should be worried what I'd do to him if I had the opportunity."

"You don't mean that."

"Try me. What can he do except rage?"

"I suppose you're right."

"All I know is, your mother should never have asked you to help me."

He slid his arm along the back of the seat. "Aside from the fact that I met you at her house in the middle of the night, she didn't have anything to do with my decision to fly you here."

She stirred in the seat. "How can you say that?"

"Because I've had to live with Vincenzo and Gemma's story for many years. The night my mother told me about *your* situation, the horror of their history came back to haunt me. For you to be forced to undergo a betrothal at your age was not only feudal, it was criminal."

"Zia Bertina said the same thing many times. That's why she agreed to help me escape. I'll love her forever for what she did for me."

"The emotional damage to you was as bad as anything physical," Cesare spoke his mind. "When Mamma asked if I would help you leave Palermo, I didn't have to think about it and was determined to help you any way I could. That hasn't changed for me. Does that answer your question?"

Once more she hid her face in her hands, but she nodded.

He ruffled one of her curls with his fingers. "You

said you wished you were a normal girl I'd hired to work in one of my restaurants in New York. In truth it's exactly what I've done, but this restaurant happens to be in Milan. Shall we put all the angst of the past aside and concentrate on tomorrow? You're my new pastry chef who's going to be running the show."

She finally lifted her head. "I intend to make you proud. Maybe you should take me back to the apartment. I rested a little today, but I didn't sleep. If I go to bed now, I'll be in much better shape by morning. Another time I'll come out here and watch for the swans."

Tuccia's resilience was something to behold.

"There'll be many opportunities." Cesare started the engine and he drove them back to the *pensione*. When they arrived, he walked her to the door.

Don't touch her, Donati.

If he made that mistake, he would never leave her apartment. "I'll be by for you at eight. We'll have a working breakfast with Gemma."

"I'll be ready. Thank you for the dinner and the tour, Cesare. *Dormi bene.*"

"*E tu.*"

Giving in to unassuaged longings, he pulled her in his arms, kissing her long and hard.

He walked back to his car aware of a new fear attacking him. How would he handle it if he asked her to marry him and she turned him down?

CHAPTER EIGHT

CESARE WOULD BE by for her in a few minutes. Tuccia stood in front of the bathroom mirror in full chef regalia. She peered through her glasses. No lipstick. Not a hair in sight. No perfume, either. Gemma had told her not to wear any, but she could use a non-scented lotion.

"This is your big day. If you're recognized by someone on the kitchen staff, then it's all over. Until then you're going to do whatever it takes to prove worthy of Cesare's faith in you."

Last night he'd pulled her in his arms and kissed her as she'd hoped. Now she was longing for the day when that happened again. Tuccia had felt his touch in every fiber of her being. She'd ached for him until she was afraid she'd never get to sleep. To her relief a miracle did happen, but only because she'd been up most of the night before.

She walked through the apartment to gather her purse and bible. This place had become her home. Hers and Cesare's. She'd never known such happiness. While she stood looking out the window, she saw his car pull up. Would her heart always palpitate with a frenzy when he came near?

Not wanting to keep him waiting, she walked outside and climbed in before he could help her. His eyes were alive as they wandered from her floppy hat and down her body clothed in white to the sensible walking shoes she'd drawn out of her suitcase. She could tell he was thinking about what she really looked like under her disguise and it sent her pulse racing.

"*Bon jornu*, Signor Donati," she said in Sicilian.

"Chef Bottaro. I've been searching a long time for you." The way he'd said it in such a husky tone gave her hope that he was letting her know he loved her. With a smile, he started the car and they took off. "There are many things I want to discuss with you, not the least of which is how you're feeling this morning."

"Like I've climbed to the top of Mount Pellegrino. There's no going back and I'm looking down at a roiling ocean, terrified to make my first jump."

Something flickered in the depths of his eyes, intriguing her. "You sound like you've done that sort of thing before."

She nodded. "When I was a lot younger and hadn't been put on as tight a leash."

His mouth tightened. "I used to climb that cliff regularly before I left for New York."

"All those ships going out to sea," she mused. "Lucky you that you could leave and fulfill your destiny."

They'd reached the summit, but this time he took another road leading around the back of the *castello* where she saw a sign that said "Staff Parking Only." He pulled to a stop and shut off the engine. Turning to her, he clasped her hand and entwined his fingers with hers.

"In case you didn't realize it yet, today you're about to fulfill yours." He leaned closer. "This is for luck, even if you don't need it." To her surprise he gave her a long hungry kiss on the lips that sent a surge of warmth through her body.

She started to kiss him back, but he eased away too soon, leaving her bereft. Then he levered himself from the driver's seat. After coming around to help her out, Cesare used a remote to let them in the rear entrance and walked her down a hall with several offices. He knocked on the last door. "Gemma?"

"Oh, good. You're here!" She opened it. But the second she saw Tuccia, she let out a small gasp. "Am I having a hallucination, or is it really you?"

Cesare gave Gemma a hug. "Allow me to introduce Nedda Bottaro, the new Sicilian executive pastry chef who's going to set a trend."

"I'll say you are." Gemma in turn gave Tuccia a hug. "I would never have known you," she whispered. "You look more sensational than Maurice, who's always immaculately turned out in the latest *haute couture* style for the well-dressed chef. When he sees you, he'll be speechless."

"Is that good or bad?"

"Definitely good after he finds his voice. Come in the office which is now going to be yours and have some breakfast I had brought in. Then we'll all go to the kitchen and I'll introduce you to everyone."

They sat down to eat and talk. Later, as Gemma was showing her what she kept in the desk drawers, Vincenzo unexpectedly appeared at the door. "Excuse me for interrupting, *cara*, but I knew you would all want to see this morning's headlines. The police have called off the search for you, Tuccia."

She almost fainted from the news. So Cesare had been right. The letter had reached Jean-Michel.

Vincenzo thrust the newspaper in her hands, but in her dazed state, she turned to Cesare. "You're the reason this has happened so fast. I'm almost afraid to believe it. Will you please read what it says?"

"If that's what you want." He put down his coffee cup. "*Sicilian Princess No Longer Missing* is the headline. Le Comte Jean-Michel Ardois of Paris has released the following information to the press: 'Princess Tuccianna Falcone Leonardi, daughter of the Marchese and Machesa di Trabia of Sicily, has sent him a letter offering her deepest apologies for having disappeared the day before their marriage and causing grief to him and his family. In her letter to the *comte*, she says that throughout their betrothal, it became clear that they weren't suited for each other. She thought about it for a long time and was convinced that they both needed to find someone else in order to be fulfilled. At the last minute she decided she had to run away to spare both of them a lifetime of unhappiness because the only reason two people marry should be for love.'"

Tuccia heard a nuance in Cesare's voice that told her he was touched by her words.

"She lives in hope he'll forgive her and that one day soon he'll find a wonderful woman deserving of his love. The princess wishes him the very best in the future and hopes that in time she too will find happiness for herself."

He broke off talking. The room had gone quiet.

At this point Cesare's gaze flicked to hers. Emotion had darkened his eyes to a deep blue color. If he but knew it, Tuccia had already found her happiness. The most wonderful man on earth stood just a few feet away from her.

Vincenzo took the newspaper from him and finished reading the article, but he too sounded emotionally affected as he read the rest. "'Her parents, the Marchese and Marchesa di Trabia, have told the press they won't give up searching for their beloved daughter. She's their only child and they're praying she's safe and will want to come home soon.'"

Tuccia lowered her head. "It's hard to believe my parents would say those words. Up to now they've thought of me as the willful, unrepentant daughter who deserves to be punished. But if Cesare's mother is to be believed, my *zia* says they are sorry for what has happened. I hardly know what to think."

"Let's be thankful you've accomplished the most important thing," Cesare murmured, sounding more subdued than she'd ever heard him. "The *comte* isn't going to come looking for you now."

She lifted her head. "You're right. It would be too humiliating for him. I really do wish him well. But it's not so easy to forgive my parents."

Vincenzo wore a sober expression. "I relate to your feelings completely, Tuccianna. That's why you'll continue to work here in that disguise and we'll do everything possible to protect you until you know it's safe."

She got up from the chair. "Thank you so much," she whispered. Tuccia needed time to comprehend all this news.

Vincenzo smiled. "I defy anyone to know it's you hiding under all that white."

"When I look in the mirror, I surprise myself," she quipped. "Thanks again to all of you for helping me. I owe you a debt of gratitude I'll never be able to repay in this life."

She looked at Gemma. "If you don't mind, I'm so keyed up with this being my first day I'd like to meet the kitchen staff and get this part of it over with."

Gemma chuckled. "It'll be my pleasure. Let's go."

Tuccia stepped past Cesare. The four of them left the office and walked down another hall to the huge, state-of-the-art kitchen filled with a dozen assistants in aprons and beanies.

Her heart almost failed her to think she was going to be the pastry chef here. At the far end she saw a man in a tall chef's hat who was busy talking to Takis. Everyone was here. Her big day had arrived.

Help.

"Come on," Gemma urged. "I'll introduce you to the head man first."

Tuccia followed her.

"Maurice Troudeau? I'd like you to meet my replacement, Nedda Bottaro."

The middle-aged French chef gave Tuccia a blank stare. Obviously he didn't know what to make of her.

She took the initiative. In her heaviest Sicilian accent she said, "It's my honor to meet you, Signor. Thanks to Signor Donati, last evening I was treated to your *fettuccini Alfredo*, which I confess is the best I have ever eaten. I'm sure the herb you put in it is a secret I would never ask you to reveal.

"But I can tell you it's just one of the reasons your

reputation has spread all the way to the tip of Sicily where I come from. They think they make the best *fettuccini Alfredo*. Not true." She swiped the backs of her fingers under her chin in a typical gesture of her Palermitan heritage to make her point.

The Frenchman eyed Gemma. "So you brought us a real Siciliana."

"To our delight, Cesare found her."

Tuccia spoke up. "It's a great honor for me. I know I'm going to need your help if you're willing, Signor Troudeau."

His gaze swerved back to her. "You can call me Maurice."

She was excited to have made that tiny break-through. "*Grazie*, Maurice. Please forgive the inter-ruption when I know you are so busy. I, too, must get myself organized."

Opening her arms, she put her palms out in front, a Sicilian gesture to indicate there was much to do. When she turned, she almost walked into Cesare.

He'd seen her gestures and his blue eyes twinkled as if to say she was doing everything right.

By now Gemma had asked the pastry assistants to assemble around them. One by one Tuccia was intro-duced to the six of them. Three men and three women from Spain, Crete, France and Italy. After she'd chat-ted with each of them for a few minutes about their backgrounds and experience, she got down to the crux of what she'd planned to say ahead of time.

"Call me Nedda. We're going to be making Sicil-ian desserts from my part of the world. Such a change from the delectable Florentine desserts created by Si-gnora Gagliardi. Everything will be different at first, but she says you are all experts so I'm happy to be working with you. Some day I'll tell you my story, but not this morning.

"Don't be afraid to ask me any questions you want. Signor Donati says we should work together like one happy family. I agree. Of course there will be little squabbles from time to time, but that it is to be expected. *Si?*"

"*Si!*" they said in a collective voice.

"He's going to give you the recipes we'll be making for the next few weeks. I'd like you to study them. *Pignolata, cassata, biancomangiare, cannoli*—so many you'll be counting them in your sleep like the proverbial sheep." Except that she hadn't made them yet and had a lot of homework to do first. Cesare had printed them out for her.

Everyone laughed.

"Tomorrow we will begin." She nodded to Cesare. "Go ahead, *signor*, while I get acquainted with this kitchen. I don't like working in such a large space and will probably want to move some things around."

Vincenzo and Takis talked with Cesare for a few minutes, then left.

While Gemma gave Tuccia a two-hour tour of her new world, she felt Cesare's gaze on her the entire time. Eventually the three of them ended back up in the office.

A tired-looking Gemma smiled at her. "I never saw anything so amazing in my life as the way you made the kitchen your own. When you rattled off all those desserts, you sounded as if you'd been making them all your life." Ha!

"I've eaten them all my life, if that counts," Tuccia interjected with a smile.

"Maurice is so dazzled by the *Siciliana* I don't think he'll ever be the same again."

"Neither will the assistants," Cesare stated. "Everyone was mesmerized beyond their ability to talk, including me. What do you say I drive you back to the *pensione*, and we'll let Gemma have her freedom."

"Of course," Tuccia exclaimed. "I can't thank you enough, but I know you need to rest."

"I'll admit I can't wait to go upstairs and lie down. But I also have to admit I'm envious of the experience you're about to have, Tuccia. With Cesare's help you really are going to turn into an outstanding chef. I just hope you won't have to leave us prematurely."

"That's the last thing I want."

"Amen," Cesare murmured. "Shall we go?"

After thanking Gemma and giving her a hug, they walked out to the car and left for the village. Tuccia felt Cesare's gaze on her. "You're very quiet all of a sudden. You must be as hungry as I am. It's after three."

"That's not it. I was thinking about the latest news. Jean-Michel will probably demand recompense from my parents for his pain. And how do I know if my parents really are sorry?"

"Time will tell. But that isn't all you need to be worried about." He'd pulled up in front of the deli.

Her head jerked around. "What do you mean?"

"You're going to have to watch out for Mario and Manoussos, the two assistants who aren't married yet. Both seem to be besotted by you."

"That's ridiculous."

"I overhead them talking in the pantry about who was going to bed the *squisita* Siciliana first."

She scoffed. "You made that up."

"I wish I had. Little do they know they'll never be able to get you alone, not when I bring you to the *castello* every morning, and take you home every night."

Tuccia loved the possessive ring she'd detected in his voice.

"Even though there are strict rules about the staff having relationships, they'll try everything in their power to persuade you to go out for lunch with them. After one success, they won't stop."

"Cesare—I don't pl—"

"I know what I'm talking about," he cut her off, "because the types in my restaurants in New York are no different when it comes to a beautiful woman. Don't say you weren't warned." He reached for the door handle. "I'll be right back."

He actually sounded upset, but that was because he felt totally responsible for her safety at this point. That meant physically and other ways, too. They'd shared a moment of intense passion, but to her chagrin she knew Cesare would never take advantage of her. Furthermore he wouldn't allow anyone else to, either.

If he only knew what was in her heart, he wouldn't give a thought to what he'd overheard. But it thrilled her to think that on his watch, he might not like the idea that she could get interested in a man she found attractive.

Manoussos, the assistant from Crete, had a rather dashing appeal in his own way. Kind of like a younger Takis. While her mind was still mulling over their conversation, Cesare came back to the car with their food and drove them to the apartment.

"Excuse me while I change out of these clothes. I'll be right back."

It was wonderful to discard the hat and stocking. Now her head could breathe. After removing her uniform and shoes, she put on jeans and a top. Once she'd run the brush through her curls, she hurried back to the kitchen. Cesare had already laid out their meal and poured the red wine they'd opened the other day.

"I can see you've bought enough *polenta* and *cotoletta alla Milanese* for half a dozen people."

"I'm partial to both."

She would have to remember that considering he was a connoisseur of fine food. After a few bites she agreed the ribs were delicious. "But I'm afraid that for me the grilled *polenta* is an acquired taste."

"Long ago it was considered the food of the poor, but I loved it when I first moved to Milan."

"My friend in Catania loves it, too. She said it reminds her of the porridge she ate when she was studying in England. I miss talking to her. She wouldn't believe it if she knew what I've been doing."

He drank the rest of his wine and sat back in the chair. "Today has marked a drastic change in your life. After nine years, you're no longer engaged to be married, releasing you from your prison. Even better, you're employed with a vitally important job and benefits."

"All because of you," she blurted.

"You don't need to keep thanking me, Tuccia." He'd turned serious all of a sudden. She hardly knew what to think. "This job is going to run your life for a while.

To make it a little easier, you're going to have to take breaks in order to handle the stress. It's time we talk about a schedule for you."

"All right."

"Basically you come to work at eight-thirty and can leave by three o'clock Monday through Friday. You'll alternate being on duty Saturday or Sunday evening twice a month from six to nine. Not to cook, but to make certain things are running smoothly."

She thought about it for a minute. "If there are problems, then I need to improvise. Is that what you're saying?"

"Should there be any issues, I'll be there to help."

"I see. But who spells you off?"

He raked a hand through his hair. "We're not talking about me."

She shouldn't have asked. Cesare was in a strange mood.

"Gemma and I worked out a schedule where she had two weekends off a month and Maurice the other two. I believe it's still the best way to arrange your time. When you're off, Maurice will handle any difficulties that come up."

"That sounds more than fair. Does it mean that you'll be taking those same weekends off?"

"Yes. That's how it has worked in the past so I can fly to New York and get my business done there."

The knowledge that he'd be gone at the same time she had two days to fill on her own private agenda was more than disappointing news. It was awful. Tuccia was so used to being with him she couldn't imagine him being so far away. To think that a week ago they hadn't even met. Now...

"Do you know how to drive, Tuccia?"

His question surprised her. "Yes. My *zia* taught me how. But I don't have a license because my parents never allowed me to have a car. Why do you ask?"

Frown lines formed around his eyes. "Always assuming you'll wear your disguise, I was going to let you use my car when I'm not in Milan. Under the circumstances, I'll make an arrangement with the limousine service so a driver will be on call for you at any time, day or night, when I'm not available. You need freedom to do the things you want and have to do."

No one in the whole world was more thoughtful than Cesare. *No one.* But in his odd frame of mind, she chose not to tell him that he didn't have to do that for her.

"Thank you. I'm very grateful for your generosity. But what would you think if we altered the daily routine a little?"

"In what way?"

"If you picked me up in the mornings, we could talk about the day ahead of me. But at three o'clock I could go home in the limo with another recipe you wanted me to make. I could get the groceries needed and do my errands. Then I'd make the dessert. When it was done, you could come by to test it. It will free up your time. What do you think?"

"It's your decision."

"I see."

If she dared, she'd ask if she could fly to New York with him. She'd traveled all over Europe under supervision, but she'd never been in New York before. Tuccia would love to see the original Mamma's, and where he'd lived before he'd put the *castello ris-torante* on the map.

"Just so you know, your first weekend off will be in two weeks, starting when three o'clock rolls around on Friday afternoon. Do you have other questions for me right now?"

Too many, especially one about how she would fill her time while he was away, but anything she wanted to ask him wasn't about her schedule and she feared he didn't want to hear it.

"No. Between you and Gemma, I'm feeling much more confident about everything."

"You were brilliant today."

"The credit goes to my teacher."

A strange silence followed before he suddenly got up from the table. "I'm afraid I have to go, but I'll be by for you at eight in the morning."

"Could you do one more favor first and buy the ingredients I need to make the pastries I've never prepared? I'll start practicing on a couple of the recipes before I go to bed."

He smiled. "I'll be right back." Twenty minutes later he returned with the items needed.

"Thank you so much, Cesare. Now don't let me keep you any longer."

He was probably so sick of teaching her how to cook his recipes he couldn't wait for some breathing space. It was only five in the afternoon and there wasn't a thing she could do about it. He'd done his duty, now he was out of there.

"Thank you for lunch," she said after following him to the door with her heart dragging on the tiles.

He gave her a heartbreaking smile, but didn't try to hold her or kiss her. "I promise, no more *polenta.*"

"It was good for me to try it. I'm a cook now and need to be open to new taste experiences from the expert himself."

"You're becoming a very fine pastry cook," he corrected her.

"*Arrivederci*, Cesare."

He nodded before getting in his car and took off like a rocket.

Trying to pull herself together, she walked back in the kitchen to clean everything up. While she worked, Cesare's words rang in her ears.

Today has marked a drastic change in your life.

No kidding. Her teacher had done his job.

She remembered something else he'd told her days ago.

There's no room in my life for any woman until the castello'*s new pastry chef can create masterpieces without my help.*

That day had come. Though they were Cesare's masterpieces, he'd decided it was time to push his needy fledgling out of the nest.

You're on your own, Tuccia. You'd better get used to it fast.

CHAPTER NINE

TUCCIA COULDN'T BELIEVE how fast the next week flew by. It didn't take her long to get into a rhythm. So far the camaraderie with her assistants was building. They were remarkably trained and skilled, hoping to become a chef at a great restaurant one day themselves.

The two guys who constantly flirted with her made the day fun, but she could never take either one of them seriously despite Cesare's reminders to be careful not to lead them on. She loved it that he was always around in the background, watching everything without being obvious about it.

Tuccia still felt a fraud at having been promoted to executive pastry chef status in a week. But the others had no idea how it had happened. With Cesare her mentor, she'd been hyper-glided into the coveted position, one that was saving her life.

Maurice liked to tease her about her Sicilian ways. Things were coming along. In truth she liked having an important reason to get up in the morning and go to work. She liked cooking! With every new dessert, she needed less help to figure it out and perfect it.

On Thursday, just before quitting time, Cesare

came in while she was testing the results of her assistants' creations in the ricotta cheesecake department. Each cook had put his or her initials on a piece of tape on the side of the pan. "This particular cake is lacking two essential ingredients that were included in the recipes I passed out." She knew who had made it. "Why don't we ask Signor Donati to tell you what they are?"

Manoussos no longer looked happy as she cut Cesare a piece and walked over to give it to him with a fork. Their gazes met in silent amusement. He started to eat. Tuccia was loving every second of this. Cesare finally put the empty plate down on the counter.

"Signorina Bottaro is right. I don't detect the strong flavor of chocolate or amaretto."

"You see," she exclaimed. "The secret of this cheesecake is to crumble amaretto cookies into the crust, and add two extra tablespoons of chocolate. Leave out either of these ingredients and it will taste like all the mediocre cheesecakes you've ever eaten."

"It was my mistake," Manoussos spoke up. "I was playing a little joke to see if you could tell. But I didn't realize Signor Donati would be doing the testing. I'm very sorry."

"I'm glad you did it and I forgive you," Tuccia said with a smile. "Now perhaps you'll take me seriously and understand the *castello ristorante* doesn't do mediocre!" She stared at all of them. "That's it for today. See you bright and early in the morning."

Cesare broke into laughter after they'd walked out to his car. "He's still upset that he can't get anywhere with you. I have it in my heart to feel sorry for him because he'll never get the chance."

That made two people who were upset because Tuccia wasn't getting anywhere with Cesare and she was in pain over it.

She loved him to the bottom of her soul. They could be together all night every night if that was what he wanted. But maybe she needed to face the cold hard fact that he didn't feel the same way about her. She didn't want to believe it, not when she was so deeply in love with him.

During the second week of her being in charge of her crew in the *castello* kitchen, Cesare had come by the apartment after work to test the chocolate *setevelli torta*, a nine-layer cake he'd taught her how to make. When he tested the end result, he told her it tasted like the food of the gods.

She smiled and thanked him. "Such praise makes a girl's head swell." In horrible pain because he wasn't being more demonstrative in an intimate way, she had to do something to end it. "Since I'm thrilled I've passed your exacting test, please feel free to leave and enjoy the rest of your evening."

For once he looked taken back. Was it shock, or could it possibly be disappointment that she'd brushed him off so fast and he didn't like it? She got excited to think it might be the latter.

"Why do I get the feeling you want me to go?"

"It's not that. If you must know, I've made plans for tonight and I don't want to put them off. The limo will be here soon."

"To do what?" he asked in a controlled voice.

Oh, Cesare—tell me what's going on inside you.

"To do some important clothes shopping in Milan."

"You could have asked me at any time. I would have taken you."

"I know you would, but I'm no longer like the in-flight helpless woman who developed an embarrassing crush on her protector during those first few days." There! She'd said it to disabuse him of any notion that he needed to worry about her any longer.

From the look of his tautened mouth, she'd found her mark. It encouraged her to go on and finish making her point. "That fairy tale has ended now that you've given me the tools to help myself. Since the police are no longer looking for me, I want to get out on my own."

"Tuccia—it's probably not a good idea for you to walk alone at the shops this time of evening. It'll be dark soon. A beautiful woman is a target for unsavory types."

"But it's what I've been wanting to do, and any woman is a target for a pickpocket. I can defend myself and I'll take my chances. To be a normal person without a bodyguard following me around sounds like heaven."

His jaw hardened. "Is that what I've become to you?"

She folded her arms, tamping down her elation that he was upset. "I'm going to forget you asked me that question. It's not worthy of you. I was referring to the security my parents hired to keep me watched day and night. Cesare—I need my freedom. Is it so inconceivable that I would want you to have yours and get on with your life the way it was before we met?"

The lids of his eyes had lowered so she couldn't read their expression.

"In fact as long as we're having this conversation, I want you to know that the salary you've put in the bank account for me will remain untouched until I've paid back every cent I owe you. Wait—" she said when he started to protest.

"I don't want to be beholden to you or anyone. Because of your incredible generosity, I've been given an option that opens many doors to my future when I no longer work here."

"You're planning on leaving us soon?" His voice sounded almost wintry.

His reaction was more than she could have asked for. If by some miracle he'd fallen in love with her, too, then she had to do something to get him to break down and tell her how he felt.

"I would never do that to you. But yesterday you told me you heard from your mother and received wonderful news. Ciro is starting to make progress. It's possible he'll be well enough to work again in a couple of months rather than six. You have to be so relieved if he's able to come back much sooner than expected."

Ignoring her comment he said, "Do you wish you could get out of our agreement sooner?" He wasn't letting this go. She prayed it was a good sign.

"No." She shook her head. "Every day I'm here I learn something new and valuable. There isn't a cook in Europe who wouldn't sell his or her soul to be the executive pastry chef in a restaurant as renowned as yours. Don't you think I know that? Until Ciro is ready to come to work, I'll do everything I can to justify your faith in me."

He stood at the door, ready to leave. "Would you rather I didn't pick you up in the mornings?"

She hadn't expected that question, but she'd done it to herself and had to live with it. "I love being picked up. Who wouldn't? But I'm sure it isn't always convenient for you. All you have to do is phone me if something comes up and I'll send for the limo." Tuccia moved closer to him. "Do you want to know what my greatest concern is?"

"I don't have to guess," he muttered. "You're talking about your aunt."

"Actually I'm not as worried now. But I'm thinking about you and the risk you took to talk your partners into helping me in the first place."

"I didn't have to go that far," he bit out. "When they heard about your situation and ate that batch of tarts you made, they wanted to protect you."

"Nevertheless I wish I could do something important for you to pay you back."

"You are," he said in a gravelly voice. "Talk among the staff is growing that your desserts have already resulted in rave reviews from our latest guests. In fact several of the top food magazines, including *Buon Appetito*, already want an interview with the new pastry chef."

"That's nice to hear, but I can't take any credit for it. The people they need to talk to are you and your mother."

He cocked his head. "Would it interest you to know that the top dessert so far is your *granita*? Maurice says it's perfection."

Tuccia adored Cesare for saying that. She loved him so terribly she was going to blurt it out if he didn't leave in the next few seconds. "Then the credit for that goes to the chef on my parents' yacht."

"Not everyone can follow a recipe the way you've done and improve it. Why won't you take credit for what you're doing?"

She averted her eyes.

A sound of exasperation came out of him. "I can see I'm not going to get the answer I'm looking for from you."

Nor I from you, my darling.

"Enjoy your evening out, but be careful. Unless there's an emergency, I'll be by at eight in the morning." He opened the door.

"Cesare?" She was dying inside.

He turned around so fast it startled her. "*Si?*"

"Would you mind answering a question for me?"

"Have I ever?"

Oh, dear, but she was determined to ask him anyway. "I was just wondering if you would consider taking me to New York with you on my first weekend off. To see it with you would mean everything to me."

"I'm afraid that would be out of the question. I have too much business and couldn't show you around."

His rejection was swift and true, cutting her to the very marrow of her bones. Tuccia would never make that mistake again. "I just thought I'd ask. I hope you have a lovely night without any worries for a change."

"That'll be the day," he ground out, "but I appreciate the thought."

It was the hardest thing she'd ever done to keep a smile on her face and pretend he hadn't destroyed her with those words. But somehow she managed to maintain her poise until he drove off.

Now that he was gone, she knew what she had to do. After he'd left and she could no longer hear the engine, Tuccia called for a taxi rather than the limo service Cesare had arranged for her to use. She didn't want her whereabouts this evening to be traced.

When it drew up to the apartment, she walked outside and exchanged greetings with the *padrona* before she got in. Once she shut the door, she asked the driver to take her to the airport and drop her off at the main terminal.

Then she sat back and contemplated what she had to do. If Cesare had been willing to take her to New York, everything would have been different. But with that dream gone, she needed to follow through on a plan growing in the back of her mind.

Before long the limo pulled up to the drop-off area. She paid the driver and got out, waving him on. Then she walked through the crowds to the ticketing counter and booked a round trip ticket from Milan to Palermo. Bless her *zia* for slipping her a little money in case of an emergency. Bertina must have been psychic!

She would leave next Friday after work, the beginning of her first weekend off, and return Sunday evening. The police weren't looking for her so she didn't worry about being spotted. If by chance any detectives her parents had hired did see her name on a passenger list and alert her parents, she'd have to deal with it then.

As soon as she'd booked both two-hour flights and had paid cash, she got another taxi and headed right back to the *pensione*. Relieved that she'd finally done something about an impossible situation, she prepared for bed and climbed under the covers.

Her plan was to take a taxi to Bertina's palazzo. Tuccia couldn't bear to put her *zia* through any more grief. They needed to talk face-to-face about everything. She needed the woman who'd been like a mother to her growing up, before she faced her parents.

Without doing that, she could never embrace the newfound independence Cesare had tried to give her at great risk to him. Whatever happened, it was time to take total charge of her life.

On the next Friday afternoon at three o'clock sharp, Cesare said good-night to Tuccia and watched her leave the *castello* in the limousine. He decided to give her an hour after she got back to her apartment before he made a surprise appearance at her door. She believed he was leaving for New York. That was what he'd wanted her to think.

Surely she knew why he'd told her she couldn't come with him when she'd asked him. She had to know he was madly in love with her.

For the last week he'd been functioning on automatic pilot and knew it couldn't go on until he got Tuccia alone. His plan was to whisk her away in his car to Lago di Garda. Italy's largest lake was situated two hours away from Milan by car. He'd booked a romantic hideaway near the picturesque town of Salo where they wouldn't be disturbed.

In three weeks she'd become his whole world and he wouldn't rest until they'd talked everything out and he'd told her what was in his heart.

He let Vincenzo know he was leaving. After he cleared the decks with Maurice, his work was finished

here. Cesare showered and packed a bag. With everything done, he took off in his car for the *pensione.*

When he walked to her door and knocked, he felt
an adrenaline rush impossible to contain. "Tuccia?
It's Cesare." He waited and listened, but didn't hear
anything. "Tuccia?" He knocked hard. "I have to talk
to you."

Nothing.

Had she already gone somewhere in the limo?

He got back in his car and called the limo service.
The dispatcher told him she'd rung for a car to pick
her up at the *castello* at three o'clock, but she hadn't
requested another limo. Cesare thanked him and hung
up, not liking the vibe he was getting.

His next thought was that she must have gone for
a walk in the village. Rather than try looking for her,
he called her cell phone, but she didn't answer. If she
was inside the apartment, he couldn't imagine her not
picking up when she saw the caller ID.

Growing more anxious, he phoned the *padrona* and
asked if she'd seen Tuccia. The older woman said the
last time she saw her was yesterday when she came
home still wearing her chef's outfit.

"Will you do me a favor and let yourself inside to
find out if she's too ill to answer the door?"

"*Naturalmente.* I will call you right back."

Cesare watched her leave her apartment and enter
Tuccia's. Suddenly she reappeared at the entrance and
waved for him to come in. At this point he broke out
in a cold sweat fearing what he would find.

He jumped out of the car and rushed inside, dread-
ing to think what he might find. But instead of Tuccia
passed out on the floor or ill in her bed, the *padrona*

handed him a sheet of paper. He could see it was lined and had come from Tuccia's bible.

"I found this on the table, *signor*. She left this for you. I will go now."

"Grazie," he murmured, feeling gutted.

After the door closed, he read what she'd written.

In case someone from the castello *tries to reach me and can't, I've gone to my* zia *in Palermo for the weekend.*

His eyes closed tightly. He squeezed the note into a ball. Pain almost debilitated him. She had to have taken a plane because a train or bus would never have gotten her there in time. Cesare knew how terrible she felt for her aunt, but he hadn't expected Tuccia to fly into the hornet's nest this soon.

Blackness had descended on him. After locking her front door, he took off for the airport in his car. The first thing he did en route was phone the pilot and alert him he needed to fly to Palermo ASAP. Next he called his mother, but she didn't answer and it went to her voice mail.

He left the message that he'd be in Palermo tonight and needed to talk to her the second he got there. Cesare had come to the low ebb of his life. He couldn't lose Tuccia.

When the taxi drove up to the gates of the palazzo at quarter to ten that night, Tuccia paid the driver and jumped out. She ran into Paolo. Her aunt's grounds-keeper looked shocked when he recognized her, and he let her through.

She put a finger to her lips. "Shh. I want to surprise my *zia*. How is she, Paolo?"

"Very, very sad and missing you. Praise the angels you have come back."

Tuccia kissed his ruddy cheek and darted up the long flower-lined walkway to the main entrance. She tugged on the door pull and waited for Adona to answer. The housekeeper never went to bed until late.

After a minute she could hear someone talking on the inside and then the door opened.

The second Adona saw her, she put her hands to her mouth in shock. "Ah! Ah! Principessa!" she cried and called out to Bertina. Her booming voice must have reached the second floor because suddenly there was Tuccia's *zia* hurrying down the staircase in her robe with her dark hair undone, to find out what was going on.

Tuccia put down her suitcase and ran toward her. They met at the bottom step. She flung her arms around the woman who'd made her life worth living.

"Mia cara ragazza." Bertina kissed her over and over again while the tears ran down her cheeks. "I've been afraid I might never see you again. My prayers have been answered."

"So have mine," Tuccia cried, kissing her cheeks once more. "I've missed you more than you will ever know. Let's go up to your room so you can get back in bed and we'll talk in comfort."

"Do you need anything? Something to eat? Drink?"

"No. I just got off the plane and had a meal in flight. The only thing I need is to have a long, long talk with you about so many things."

With their arms hooked, they climbed the staircase where she'd rushed up and down so many times growing up. She could have found Bertina's boudoir wearing a blindfold. The room smelled like her lemon perfume, bringing back so many memories.

"Come on. I want you to get back in bed. You've had a great shock. I'll sit right here beside you and we'll catch up. Shall I ask Adona to bring you some tea?"

"No, no. I don't want to bother her."

Tuccia helped her off with her robe and puffed the pillows. Then her *zia* leaned back and pulled up the covers. "I just want to look at my beautiful daughter for a little while. You *are* my daughter, even if my sister gave birth to you."

"You already know how I feel about you." She kissed her forehead. "Ever since I ran away, I've worried about you until I've been ill over it."

"I've been all right. Over the last few days I've had several long talks with your mother who is suffering over what has happened. We're not sisters for nothing, and I know she has a sorrow in her heart until she can make peace with you."

"Then it's true what you told Lina?"

"Of course. She and your father, though he doesn't show it, were frightened when they thought you'd been kidnapped. It was one of those life-changing experiences for them. I don't believe they're the same people from before."

"So you believe what was printed in the newspaper?"

"Yes. They miss you and want you to come home. I'm convinced of it."

Tuccia stared into her eyes. "I want to believe it."

"I think that if you call them and have a talk, you'll find they're full of regrets, especially for the cruel betrothal forced on you, and they want a fresh start. You don't have to do it, of course."

"No. I want to do it, Zia. That's why I'm here."

She clapped her hands. "My prayers have been answered."

"Mine, too. If it hadn't been for Cesare's mother keeping him informed so he could tell me how you are, I would have lost my mind."

"Lina has become my close friend and has been a great blessing in my life."

Tuccia held her hand. "You have no idea *how* great, Zia."

Bertina heard the inflection in her voice. "Tell me what you mean."

"Do you know where I've been for the last three weeks?"

"No. I only know her son flew you to Milan so you could get away."

"There's so much to tell you I don't know where to start."

"At the beginning!" Bertina squeezed Tuccia's hand hard, causing her to chuckle. "Do you know that even though you've had to live through such a terrible ordeal, you seem happy. I don't think it's just because you're free of that deplorable engagement. I detect a glow about you."

"You do?"

"Yes. Your eyes are alive, like you've come out of a deep sleep. What's going on?"

"Did Lina tell you that the chef her son had hired

for the *castello ristorante* had gone to the hospital the same night she let me stay at her villa?"

"Oh, yes. We've both been to visit him at the hospital." Tuccia didn't know that.

"But she hasn't told you anything else?"

"Only that he found a place for you to stay in Milan."

"At a *pensione* in a village at the base of the *castello.*"

"So you didn't have to leave Milan. It sounds like he was very good to you."

She took a big breath. "I'm afraid good doesn't begin to cover what he has done for me. What I'm about to tell you is going to come as a huge shock."

Bertina looked at her in that amazing way she had of reading between the lines. Tuccia had never been able to keep secrets from her, not that she'd wanted to. "Why do I get the feeling that the devilishly handsome Cesare Donati is more involved in all this than I had imagined?"

She bit her lip. "I'm in love with him, Zia! Wildly, passionately in love."

Her brows lifted. "Have you been living with him?"

"Not in the way you mean. I *wish* he'd asked me to live with him."

"Tuccianna—"

"That may sound terrible to you, but it's how I feel. We've been together every day and I've never known such joy in my life."

Bertina nodded. "Is he in love with you, too?"

She looked down. "I don't know. I think he is—I pray he is."

"You mean he hasn't told you?"

"No."

"Nor you him?"

"I couldn't! Our relationship hasn't been like that. One night he started kissing me and I thought I would die from happiness, but since then he hasn't tried to make love to me. I'm still trying to figure out why. I think he loves me, but—"

"You only think?" the older woman laughed.

"Unless I don't understand men and have been reading everything wrong."

"Why don't you start again, slowly, and give me a minute-by-minute explanation of what you've been up to that has turned you into a different person? Don't withhold any details. Together we just might figure everything out."

"I want to do that, but first I need to talk to my parents."

"Why don't I call them and tell them to come over here now."

"You think they'll come this late?"

Bertina shook her head. "If you only knew how much they've missed you, you wouldn't have to ask that question."

While Tuccia sat there trembling, she listened to the brief conversation. When her *zia* hung up, she said, "They're coming this instant. Why don't you freshen up and meet them at the door?"

"Will you come down with me?"

"No, my darling girl. This is a conversation you need to have with them alone. It's been twenty-five years in coming."

After going the bedroom she always used here, Tuccia hurried downstairs and waited until she heard the bell pull outside the door. When she opened it and saw her parents standing there, she was stunned by the rush of emotions that bombarded her.

"Tuccianna—" her mother cried and ran to embrace her. "You've come back. I was so afraid we would never see you again." They hugged for a long time.

After they broke apart, she looked at her father. "Papa?"

"Figlia mia." Tears poured down his cheeks. For the first time she could remember, he reached out and hugged her so hard she could barely breathe, but she didn't care. "Forgive us," he cried and broke down sobbing.

"Let's all go in the salon," she said, putting her arms through both of theirs. Once in the other room they sat down on the couch. She pulled up a chair so she could be close and look at them. Gone were the severe expressions of two people who'd been so rigid.

"I'm the one who's sorry for doing something so terrible, for frightening you and embarrassing you and Jean-Michel. But I couldn't marry him. I just couldn't!"

Her mother nodded. "I knew that the moment you'd disappeared from the bridal shop. I don't think I'll ever get over the shame of forcing you into an engagement that ruined your life for years. Bertina made us see how wrong we've been."

"We didn't mean to hurt you, Tuccianna," her father murmured in the saddest voice she'd ever heard. "While you've been gone, we've learned some things about Jean-Michel that let us know he would never have made you a good husband. You don't ever have to worry about him again. We've been so blind. How can we make this up to you?"

"By accepting me for who I am, and accepting the most wonderful man on earth whom I hope to marry."

"You've met someone?" her mother cried.

"Yes. Cesare Donati. I'm terribly in love with him. He came to my rescue the day I ran away. We've been together ever since. Let me tell you about him. About us."

For the next little while she related her experiences, leaving nothing out. "I'm now the executive pastry chef at the *castello* in Milan. I can't wait for you to meet him. You already know his wonderful mother."

"We do?"

"Yes, Mamma. She's Zia Bertina's cook."

Her father's eyes widened. "Lina Donati?"

She nodded. "Bertina asked her to hide me at her villa that first night, and I bumped into Cesare. It was love at first sight for me. But I don't know what's going to happen now." Tuccia knew he'd tried to be so careful with her to honor her because that was the way he was made. But she needed to know why he wouldn't take her to New York. They had to talk.

"We want you to be happy, Tuccia," her father declared.

"That's all we want." Her mother had broken down in tears again. "Will you let us be a part of your lives?"

Overjoyed to hear that question, she flew off the chair and embraced both of them.

CHAPTER TEN

THIS TIME WHEN Cesare arrived at the villa near midnight, his mother was up to greet him. They hugged before he followed her into the kitchen. She'd made his favorite *tarelli* lemon biscuits and her own version of espresso.

"I was at the hospital when I got your message and hurried home. You'll be pleased to know Ciro is making amazing strides. I think he might be released from the hospital sooner than anyone expected."

Cesare let out a deep sigh. "That news couldn't come at a better time." He had plans for him and Tuccia.

"It's clear you have something serious to say to me, Cesare. Tell me what has happened for you to show up like this late at night in such a frantic state."

They sat around the kitchen table while he drank his coffee. "I'm afraid you're going to be shocked when I tell you. I'm in love with Tuccia Leonardi."

She leaned forward on the table and eyed him seriously. "I've been wondering when you would finally tell me about what you did with her. What's wrong?"

"She left Milan without telling me. I'm terrified I might have lost her. If the worst has happened, I don't know how I'm going to live without her. Mamma, how did you handle it when Papa left you? I can't comprehend it."

His mother reached for his hand. "Where did that question come from?"

"I guess from the time I heard you crying in the bedroom when I was six. You were looking at his picture."

She squeezed his fingers before letting him go. "You thought I was crying about him. I wish I'd known. I could have saved you years of grief."

"What do you mean?"

"My tears over him had been shed long before he ever left. He didn't want marriage or responsibility. When I realized how unhappy we both were living together, I asked him to leave."

Cesare frowned. "You asked him?"

"Yes."

"So he didn't just walk out?"

"No. But I knew he wanted to and so I gave him his freedom. The day you saw me in tears, I was crying because he never did come back to see you and Isabella. You deserved a wonderful father and I could only be your mother. But I thank God every day he was your father because I have the two most wonderful children on earth. Now tell me why you think you've lost her?"

"Tuccia's my life, but when I went to her apartment earlier today, she'd gone. There was a note that said she'd flown here to see Bertina."

"Does she know how you feel about her?"

"Not in so many words."

"Because she's a princess?"

"I don't know. Maybe I've felt I wasn't good enough for her."

"Nonsense! My brilliant son. You're as blind as a bat where the *principessa* is concerned. Now let's really talk."

He sucked in his breath. "There's a lot you don't know. Without telling me, Tuccia flew here on her own."

His mother eyed him curiously. "How come you know so much about what the princess does? What have you been keeping from me?"

"A lot."

She smiled in that irritating way that said she'd already figured everything out. "You fell in love with her when you whisked her away to Milan without Ciro on board."

"I'm afraid I did more than that." He had her complete attention now.

"What man with blood in his veins wouldn't have done the same thing? Bertina and I have often said it's sinful how beautiful she is. Her parents did a cruel thing forcing that betrothal on her, but it has protected her. Until *I* interfered," she added. "So what did you do?"

"I made her the pastry chef at the *castello* in order to hide her."

A laugh escaped. "You mean a kitchen helper."

"No. She's the chef who has replaced Ciro and has been for two weeks."

"With your partners' approval?"

"Yes."

"Did she even know how to cook?"

"Not when she started."

"I presume you've been teaching her everything you know."

He nodded. "Except for an exceptional *gratina* she'd learned how to make years ago by watching the cook on her parents' yacht."

"I told you she was resourceful. I take it you've forgiven me for asking you to help her get away."

Cesare sat back in the chair. "I want to marry her, Mamma."

"At last you've found a woman who's your equal."

"But—"

"But nothing! Do you imagine for one single second she would have begged you to teach her if she weren't halfway in love with you by the time you arrived in Milan? She's known her own mind for years. When she met the man meant for her, she did whatever she could to get you to fall in love with her."

That was what he'd wanted to believe. "She's beyond wonderful."

"I know, and I can't tell you how delighted I am."

"In that case, I need a big favor from you. Will you call Bertina right now? Tell her I found out Tuccia is with her. Ask them to come for breakfast first thing in the morning. Tell her this has to do with Tuccia's parents and it's absolutely vital. But don't let her know I'm here. I'll do the rest."

He waited while she reached for the phone and made the call. "Bertina?" she said, putting it on speaker. "Forgive me for disturbing you this late, but this is an emergency. I've had word that Tuccia is with you."

"Oh, Lina—she arrived earlier tonight. I'm so happy I think I'm dreaming!"

"I can only imagine your joy at seeing her again. But before anything else happens, you must bring her to my villa first thing in the morning."

"Why? What's wrong?"

"There's something of great significance going on you don't know about. We have to talk, Bertina. I wouldn't ask this of you if I weren't frightened for both of you."

"After all you did for me, of course we'll be there."

Cesare's mother smiled at him in in relief. "Good. I'm looking forward to seeing Tuccia again."

"There's so much I have to tell you. We'll come early."

The second she hung up, Cesare shot out of the chair and walked around to hug her.

At eight in the morning, Tuccia and her aunt left the palazzo in a limo. Once again she found herself being driven through the streets to Mondello, one of the poshest areas of the city.

Before Tuccia had gone to bed in the suite she always used, Bertina had phoned to tell her about the conversation with Cesare's mother. She'd insisted she had some news they needed to hear.

Her heart thumped with sickening speed. The only way anyone knew she'd flown to Palermo tonight was through Cesare. But that meant he'd had to go to her apartment and find the note she'd left. Since he didn't have a key, he would have been forced to ask the *padrona* for help if he thought something was wrong. Why had he bothered?

She'd thought he'd flown to New York after they'd said goodbye. Evidently he'd dropped by the *pensione* before leaving for the airport. There'd been a phone call from him while she'd been on her way to the airport in the taxi, but she'd turned her phone off. Though she could have answered it—had wanted to respond—she was trying to keep her distance.

Had he phoned his mother because he was worried her parents would try to prevent her from returning to Milan? Surely he knew she would never allow that to happen. Tuccia had made a contract with him, one she would never break. How could he think she wouldn't return on Sunday night to fulfill her obligations?

But maybe he still saw her as a young woman who'd been so sheltered she'd be unable to stand on her own once she faced her parents. That was crazy. All she wanted in life was to be his wife. Nothing else could ever satisfy her.

"We're here, Tuccianna."

"I'm nervous, Zia. What do you imagine Lina needs to tell us that's so important?"

"I don't know, but I trust her with my life."

Just the way Tuccia trusted her son.

They got out of the limo and walked to the villa entrance. When the door opened, Tuccia expected to see Lina. Instead she let out a gasp and came close to a faint. *"Cesare—"*

His blue gaze traveled over her, missing nothing. "Won't you both come in? It's good to see you, Bertina." He kissed her on both cheeks. "Mamma is waiting for you in the kitchen where she has breakfast ready. Tuccia and I will join you in a few minutes, but first we have some unfinished business to talk over."

Bertina had been to the villa many times before

and walked down the hallway to the kitchen without needing directions.

Tuccia stayed where she was, glued to the spot. "What are you doing here? I thought you'd flown to New York."

"That's what I wanted you to think while I worked out a plan to take you away to a place where we could be private. But when I got to the apartment, you'd gone.

Like a fool I've given you too much time and space, but that's over. Come on. We need to be alone."

To her joy he reached for her hand and walked her up the stairs. She followed him down a hallway to what had to be his suite. After he shut the door, he lounged against it and grasped her upper arms.

"Let's get something straight right now. I only flew after you for one reason. It's the only reason I took you to Milan in the beginning. Since running into a princess in a yellow robe three weeks ago, it's the reason why I've been turned inside out and upside down. I'm in love with you, Tuccia, but you already know that. The question is, are you in love with me?"

"Oh, Cesare—" She couldn't believe what she was hearing. "How can you even ask me that? I'd fallen in love with you by the time the ducal jet landed at Milan airport. You're all I think or live for. I need you more than you will ever know."

They both moaned as he pulled her against him and he started kissing her the way he'd done at the apartment. Tuccia lost track of time as she tried to show him how much he meant to her. His mouth was doing such incredible things to her she burned with desire for him. To her joy she no longer had to hold back. He loved her!

Somehow they ended up on his bed where they began to devour each other. After three weeks of starvation, she realized she had absolutely no self-control, but she didn't care. This incredible man loved her and was making her feel immortal.

Yet Cesare was the one to call a halt before they got too carried away. He slowly relinquished her mouth and looked down at her. His eyes burned with love for her. "We're not alone in this villa and there are two people waiting for us to join them."

"I know."

"Before we go down, I have something else to say. I want to marry you as soon as possible."

"I want that, too."

"We'll make it work and live at the apartment until Ciro can come to the *castello*."

"I love the apartment. To me it's been like our little home. I'd be happy living with you there forever."

"I've felt the same way. Though I haven't dared touch you and you know why, cooking and eating together have been the highlights of my life."

"Mine, too."

"I need to meet your parents and tell them our intentions while we're here in Palermo."

"They already know my intentions."

"So you've seen them already?"

"Yes. I was with them tonight at Bertina's. It's true that they've become different people. We hugged and kissed and they can't wait to meet the man I told them I planned to marry. I'm free to live my own life and

I love you for helping me find the courage to face them."

He kissed her mouth. "I love you so much I can't live without you."

"I've been waiting to hear you say that!" she cried for joy.

"You're an amazing, loving woman. If it's all right with you, we'll go see them together so I can ask for your hand."

"They're old-fashioned and will love it."

He held her tighter. "If I have you, I have everything."

"I love you, Cesare. Way too much." She kissed each masculine feature of his striking face before kissing his mouth over and over again.

"There's something else we have to talk about. I'm anxious to plan our wedding. It needs to take place as soon as possible, or I won't be able to stand it," he whispered.

"It's all I've thought about since I met you."

"By some miracle I've found the woman for me."

"I feel the same way about you and can't belong to you soon enough."

"Two weeks from this weekend is your next time off. Our marriage can take place then. I would like Gemma and Vincenzo to be there, but I doubt they'll be able to. Still, I'm not waiting any longer to make you my wife.

"Depending on your parents' wishes, we'll have it performed in my church here, or in yours. We'll return to Milan Sunday night and take a honeymoon later after Ciro is back at the *castello*."

She ran her hands through his hair. "We'll have to

make as many arrangements as we can while we're here, but I don't want a big wedding. Just a few family friends."

"I love the way you think because I'd prefer a quiet wedding too, Tuccia." He gave her a long hungry kiss. "Now much as I don't want to leave this room, I think we'd better go downstairs to the kitchen. My mother and Bertina are dying to know what has been going on."

"I'm pretty sure they know exactly." She kissed his hard jaw, loving the taste and feel of him.

"It'll be fun to make their day."

She laughed. "I know it will."

They had trouble letting each other go. When she got up from the bed, she felt positively dizzy. "I need to fix myself first." She opened her purse and got out her styling brush.

Cesare took it from her and started running it through her curls. "I've been wanting to do this forever. But don't put on any lipstick yet. I need another kiss from you before I can go anywhere."

She threw her arms around his neck and kissed him so passionately that they wove in place. "I've ached to do this since we went to the park. I almost pulled you down and begged you to make love to me. Every time you said good-night to me and walked out without holding me in your arms, I could hardly bear it."

"In two weeks we won't ever have to suffer again. We'll be together day and night."

"By night I'll be Signora Donati. By day I'll be Nedda Bottaro."

He shook his head. "Once we've said our vows, you'll be my wife in the kitchen, too, and you'll wear whatever clothes you feel like wearing. Manoussos will be in pain when he finds out the truth."

They left the room and started down the stairs. "No he won't. You're being silly."

"Trust me. I'm a man and I know these things."

She turned to him when they reached the foyer. "Oh—I know you're a man. The most wonderful man who ever lived. Kiss me again, Cesare."

Ten days later, while Tuccia was checking the last of the desserts for the evening meal, Cesare reappeared after being gone most of her work day. Every time she sensed his presence, her heart almost burst out of her chest.

It was almost three o'clock. She'd never known him to be away from the kitchen this long. He walked over to her with a gleam in his eyes. "I'd squeeze your waist if I could find it," he teased.

Tuccia chuckled. She'd been so happy since their return from Palermo, she felt like she'd been floating. Her parents were both so impressed with Cesare that they'd given the two of them their blessing and hadn't found fault with anything. Not now that she'd come home to them.

The wedding at her family's church would be going ahead on Saturday. That day couldn't come soon enough for Tuccia.

"Guess who's in labor and has been in the hospital since eight this morning?"

"Gemma? Oh, I'm so excited for her! How's Vincenzo?"

"A complete wreck. The doctor told him it could take a long time because it's her first baby. I stayed with him as long as I could. Now Dimi and his wife are there. Takis and Lys are on their way from Crete on the jet. I'll drive you home to change and then we'll go over to the hospital."

Before long she said good-night to everyone. Cesare gathered some sandwiches in a bag and hustled her out of the kitchen to the car. When they reached the apartment, she got out of her uniform and changed into a skirt and blouse in record time.

"You look fabulous. Three more days before our world changes." He gave her a long, hungry kiss, then they left for the hospital in Milan. Everyone had gathered round in the hospital lounge. They talked about the coming wedding. It was going to be a very small morning ceremony of twenty people with a brunch afterward at the palazzo of Tuccia's parents.

Afterward she and Cesare planned to fly to Milan and spend Saturday night and Sunday at Lago di Garda before returning to their apartment. That was the place where he'd planned to take her the evening he'd come by the apartment and had found her gone. So much had happened since that night.

While they were chatting, a nurse walked toward them. "Signor Gagliardi says for you to come. If you'll follow me."

Cesare grasped her hand and they walked through the swinging doors to the second room down the hall. When they entered the room, Tuccia's breath caught. There was Gemma holding a baby in her arms with a cap of black hair. She was beaming. An exhausted-looking Vincenzo sat next to her. Both were examining their new arrival.

The proud father looked up at them. "Come all the

way in and meet our baby. We've decided to call him Nico. He's seven pounds six ounces and measures twenty-two inches long. Though he came two weeks early, the pediatrician says he's perfect."

"Felicitazioni!" sounded their cry. "A new Duc di Lombardi has graced our world."

Soon they left the hospital. She kissed Cesare's cheek. "That's a perfect family."

He reached for her hand. "That's what we're going to have, Tuccia."

"I know we're not even married yet, but already I want your baby."

"There's one promise I'll make to you. I'll do my best to get you pregnant."

"I'll do my best to get pregnant," Tuccia gave a happy sigh. "Everything has worked out because of you, Cesare."

His hand slid to her thigh. "I don't think you have any idea how much I love you."

Her heart was too full to talk. All she could do was cover his hand with her own.

"Takis seems to be handling his wife's pregnancy well," he said, "but he can be inscrutable at times. I would imagine that deep down he's holding his breath until she delivers."

After they reached the apartment and he took her inside, he pulled her down on the couch so they half lay together. "I've made a decision about something and wanted to talk it over with you."

"What is it?" But being this close, she couldn't resist kissing him again and again.

"I'm going to sell all my business interests in New York and invest the profits. I don't want to have to fly there anymore and leave you. Our life is here. We always have a place to stay at the *castello*, and at the villa when we visit my mother. But I'd like to think about a home of our own in Palermo."

"I'm so glad you said that. It's what I want. Our own place. It doesn't have to be big. Just large enough to hold two or three children. I want us to have a normal life."

"I want the same thing. You know Takis has worked things out so he can be here part of the time. The rest of the time he spends with Lys at their home in Crete. And Vincenzo lives in a villa on Lake Como with Gemma. There's no reason we can't do the same thing and fly back and forth when it's necessary."

"I think you've just made me the happiest bride-to-be in the whole world. Please don't go home tonight. Stay with me."

He hugged her tighter. "I'd like to take you in the bedroom, lock the door and throw away the key forever. Don't tempt me. Just three more days to wait, *amore mio*. We're almost there."

CHAPTER ELEVEN

CESARE STOOD AT the front of the church in Palermo with Dimi and Takis. They all wore dark blue dress suits and ties with a white rose in the lapels. He'd put the rings in his pocket. Even though Vincenzo couldn't make it, this made four times that they'd celebrated each other's weddings.

Six weeks ago, if anyone had told him he'd be married to the love of his life this morning, he would have laughed in disbelief. He kept looking at the back of the church, waiting for Tuccia to enter on the arm of her father.

The *marchesa* and her sister Bertina sat together by Cesare's mother. Behind them sat Isabella and her husband, Tomaso. They'd left the baby with Tomaso's mother. Filippa, Dimi's wife, and Lys sat by each other. The few other guests were the close friends of Tuccia's parents.

She'd insisted on keeping their wedding as low key as possible. Her life growing up had been filled with too many bad memories. She'd begged for simplicity and a non-princess wedding. Cesare had seen to her wishes.

As he wondered if something had gone wrong, he

saw the priest out of the corner of his eye. Behind him walked Tuccia on her father's arm. She looked a vision in a full-length white silk wedding dress. The lace mantilla covering her gorgeous black curls was a sight he'd never forget. She held a bouquet of white roses from her aunt's garden.

The priest had agreed to perform their short ceremony in Sicilian.

"Cesare Donati, please take Princess Tuccianna Falcone Leonardi by the hand and repeat after me."

Their eyes met before he grasped it. The love and trust in those gray orbs melted him on the spot. Thus began the age-old ritual that took on indescribable meaning to him as he kept looking at the woman who'd agreed to marry him. There was no person more precious to him.

They exchanged vows and rings.

"I now pronounce you man and wife. In the name of the Father, the Son and the Holy Spirit."

The priest didn't have to tell him to kiss his bride. Cesare gathered her in his arms and embraced her. Her hunger for him matched his. They were on fire for each other. If he could run away with her now, he would, but they had one more celebration to get through.

Holding her hand tightly, he walked her down the aisle to the foyer where everyone hugged and congratulated them. Afterward they went outside to get in the limos that drove them to her parents' palazzo for their wedding brunch on the east patio.

While they ate, Tuccia's father made an announcement. "Unbeknownst to Tuccianna and her new husband, I've made arrangements for them to have a small honeymoon aboard our yacht, so they won't be flying back to Milan for a few days."

Cesare's heart leaped. They wouldn't have to endure a flight. At least not for a couple of days.

At that juncture Takis rose to his feet. "No man should have to worry about getting back to work right away. Maurice knows about your marriage and has agreed to run the kitchen until the Siciliana gets back. He told me to tell you he's looking forward to seeing the new Signora Donati without your uniform and that floppy chef's hat."

Everyone laughed, but Tuccia's face went crimson. Cesare loved it.

"How soon can we leave?" he whispered near her ear.

"As soon as I change. I'll be right back."

She gave him a wife's kiss to torture him and hurried through the rooms to the upstairs. Once she'd gotten out of her wedding dress, she put on a pale pink summer suit and strappy high heels. Grabbing the case she'd packed earlier, she hurried back down. More hugs and kisses ensued.

But his impatience was too great. He put his arm around her shoulders, waved goodbye to everyone and they rushed outside to get in the limo. What an amazing experience to be headed for the dock in Mondello and go aboard the royal yacht.

Cesare had seen it out in the harbor many times along with the other yachts after he'd hiked the bluff. When he'd been younger all his thoughts had been intent on leaving for New York to make his way in the world. Little did he dream that his great adventure would bring him right back home, right to this yacht where his new wife had learned to make *granita*.

The deck steward showed them to the master bedroom below deck. Once he left them alone Cesare picked Tuccia up in his arms and twirled her around. "Finally I have you all to myself the way I've dreamed."

"I've had the same dreams. Love me, Cesare." Her voice shook.

"As if you need to ask me." He carried her to the bed and followed her down. They started to kiss, one after another until there was no beginning and no end. "I'm so hungry for you, I'm afraid I'll eat you alive."

"I'm afraid you won't," she cried, feverish with longing.

"*Amata.* You're so beautiful I can hardly breathe. My adorable, precious, beloved wife."

Those words were still part of her euphoria when she woke up during the night. They'd made love for hours, only to fall asleep, then start the whole heavenly process over again when they came awake.

She'd tried to imagine what it would be like to really love a man. But nothing could have prepared her for the kind of love showered on her by her new husband. There were no words to describe the ecstasy that had her clinging to him throughout the night.

At one point her rapture was so great she wept.

"What is it?" he cried.

"I was just thinking. What if I hadn't run away? What if your mother hadn't let me stay overnight? I might have missed *you.*" She moaned.

He buried his face in her neck. "Don't even think about it."

"I can't help it. I'm too happy, Cesare. No woman could ever be as happy as I am."

"You're supposed to be when you've found the right person to love. *Ti amo*, Tuccia. This is only the beginning."

Two years later, the Castello di Lombardi

Tuccia followed little Cesare around on the grass behind the *castello* near the ruins of the fourteenth-century church. Their little brown-haired son had just turned a year old, but was still unsteady on his feet. Filippa and Dimi's little dark-haired boy, Dizo, was just two months older, but handled himself with amazing agility. Her gaze followed two year-old Nico around. He was Vincenzo's clone.

Cesare came up behind her and put his arms around her waist, nuzzling her neck. "It's hilarious out here with all the children running around on the grass. Look how Nico runs after Zoe. She's the image of her mother."

"Lys is a beauty, and I can tell Zoe is going to be a heartbreaker, too, when she grows up," Tuccia said, eyeing the two-year-old with a smile.

"I think she has already stolen Nico's heart."

Tuccia turned around and gave her husband a long, passionate kiss. "Wouldn't it be amazing if they grew up loving each other?"

"You mean like Gemma and Vincenzo? It wouldn't surprise me."

"I love having a birthday picnic for all of them. Maurice and Ciro have really outdone themselves for this celebration."

"He doesn't make pastry as good as yours, my love."

"Of course he does, Cesare. Doesn't Gemma have the best ideas? This is so fun! Uh-oh. Cesare fell down."

He kissed her cheek. "I'll go get him."

Tuccia joined the women sitting on the blanket while she watched her gorgeous husband run after their son. As far as she was concerned, this was heaven.

The men were tending the children to give the women a break. All the women except Tuccia were pregnant again. Gemma was seven months along with a girl this time.

"Is Vincenzo as freaked out this time around?" Lys wanted to know.

"He's not nearly as bad as he was the first time."

"Thank heaven," Filippa exclaimed. They all laughed.

Gemma raised herself up on one elbow. "Do you know what's really strange? To be out here on the same grass where I played as a little girl with Vincenzo and Dimi. Sometimes they had sword fights."

"Who won?" Filippa wanted to know.

"They were both pretty fierce and equally matched. One time when it was Vincenzo's birthday, my mother made a little cake for him and I brought it out to him."

Tuccia smiled. "Did you always love him?"

"Always."

"And soon you were making cakes."

"And then I met Filippa at cooking school."

Tuccia stretched out. "I can't believe how lucky I was to meet Cesare. I fell so hard for him I actually learned how to make his mother's pastry in order to be near him."

"Are you taking my name in vain again?" a deep familiar voice sounded behind her. The girls chuckled.

She rolled over and looked up at him holding their son. "Afraid so. We were just saying how lucky we are to be married to such remarkable men."

Cesare's smile melted her on the spot. "Funny. The guys and I were just having the same conversation about the superb women in our lives. It all happened one morning in Vincenzo's New York apartment when he asked if Takis and I wanted to go into business with him and Dimi across the water." He stared into her eyes. "And here we are. Life truly is more fantastic and wonderful than fiction."

"I agree, Cesare." *I love you*, Tuccia mouthed the words before getting to her feet. "Come on. Let's go back to the hotel room and put little Cesare down for a nap. I want some alone time with my husband."

They hurried inside the *castello* to the private wing on the second floor. After putting their sleepy boy down, they went in their bedroom. Tuccia started to take off her clothes, unable to wait until she held Cesare in her arms.

He removed his faster and within seconds he pulled her down on the bed. *"Bellissima?"* he whispered against her lips. "Do you still love me as much as you did when we got married?"

She heard a hint of anxiety his voice.

"My darling husband, how can you even ask me that?" Except that she *did* know why. His mother had confided in her about his father. "Listen to me." She leaned over him, cupping his face in her hands.

"You're stuck with me forever. I'm never going anywhere. You're my whole life! It began the moment you crushed me in your arms. I've never told you this before, but I'm telling you now. That magical night, I felt like you'd imprinted yourself on my heart and soul. When you turned on the lights, there stood the most gorgeous man my eyes had ever beheld."

Cesare kissed her until they were both out of breath. "It was a magical night. You looked like an enchanted princess escaping her bottle."

"That's how it felt, and there you were. I love you, Cesare. Never doubt it for an instant."

"Never again, *amorada*. Never again."

* * * * *

If you missed the first two books, check out the rest of THE BILLIONAIRES' CLUB *trilogy!*

RETURN OF HER ITALIAN DUKE
BOUND TO HER GREEK BILLIONAIRE

And if you enjoyed this story, check out these other great reads from Rebecca Winters

THE BILLIONAIRE'S PRIZE
THE BILLIONAIRE WHO SAW HER BEAUTY
THE BILLIONAIRE BABY SWAP
HIS PRINCESS OF CONVENIENCE

All available now!

MILLS & BOON®
Hardback – October 2017

ROMANCE

Claimed for the Leonelli Legacy	Lynne Graham
The Italian's Pregnant Prisoner	Maisey Yates
Buying His Bride of Convenience	Michelle Smart
The Tycoon's Marriage Deal	Melanie Milburne
Undone by the Billionaire Duke	Caitlin Crews
His Majesty's Temporary Bride	Annie West
Bound by the Millionaire's Ring	Dani Collins
The Virgin's Shock Baby	Heidi Rice
Whisked Away by Her Sicilian Boss	Rebecca Winters
The Sheikh's Pregnant Bride	Jessica Gilmore
A Proposal from the Italian Count	Lucy Gordon
Claiming His Secret Royal Heir	Nina Milne
Sleigh Ride with the Single Dad	Alison Roberts
A Firefighter in Her Stocking	Janice Lynn
A Christmas Miracle	Amy Andrews
Reunited with Her Surgeon Prince	Marion Lennox
Falling for Her Fake Fiancé	Sue MacKay
The Family She's Longed For	Lucy Clark
Billionaire Boss, Holiday Baby	Janice Maynard
Billionaire's Baby Bind	Katherine Garbera

MILLS & BOON®
Large Print – October 2017

ROMANCE

Sold for the Greek's Heir	Lynne Graham
The Prince's Captive Virgin	Maisey Yates
The Secret Sanchez Heir	Cathy Williams
The Prince's Nine-Month Scandal	Caitlin Crews
Her Sinful Secret	Jane Porter
The Drakon Baby Bargain	Tara Pammi
Xenakis's Convenient Bride	Dani Collins
Her Pregnancy Bombshell	Liz Fielding
Married for His Secret Heir	Jennifer Faye
Behind the Billionaire's Guarded Heart	Leah Ashton
A Marriage Worth Saving	Therese Beharrie

HISTORICAL

The Debutante's Daring Proposal	Annie Burrows
The Convenient Felstone Marriage	Jenni Fletcher
An Unexpected Countess	Laurie Benson
Claiming His Highland Bride	Terri Brisbin
Marrying the Rebellious Miss	Bronwyn Scott

MEDICAL

Their One Night Baby	Carol Marinelli
Forbidden to the Playboy Surgeon	Fiona Lowe
A Mother to Make a Family	Emily Forbes
The Nurse's Baby Secret	Janice Lynn
The Boss Who Stole Her Heart	Jennifer Taylor
Reunited by Their Pregnancy Surprise	Louisa Heaton

MILLS & BOON®
Hardback – November 2017

ROMANCE

The Italian's Christmas Secret	Sharon Kendrick
A Diamond for the Sheikh's Mistress	Abby Green
The Sultan Demands His Heir	Maya Blake
Claiming His Scandalous Love-Child	Julia James
Valdez's Bartered Bride	Rachael Thomas
The Greek's Forbidden Princess	Annie West
Kidnapped for the Tycoon's Baby	Louise Fuller
A Night, A Consequence, A Vow	Angela Bissell
Christmas with Her Millionaire Boss	Barbara Wallace
Snowbound with an Heiress	Jennifer Faye
Newborn Under the Christmas Tree	Sophie Pembroke
His Mistletoe Proposal	Christy McKellen
The Spanish Duke's Holiday Proposal	Robin Gianna
The Rescue Doc's Christmas Miracle	Amalie Berlin
Christmas with Her Daredevil Doc	Kate Hardy
Their Pregnancy Gift	Kate Hardy
A Family Made at Christmas	Scarlet Wilson
Their Mistletoe Baby	Karin Baine
The Texan Takes a Wife	Charlene Sands
Twins for the Billionaire	Sarah M. Anderson

MILLS & BOON®
Large Print – November 2017

ROMANCE

The Pregnant Kavakos Bride	Sharon Kendrick
The Billionaire's Secret Princess	Caitlin Crews
Sicilian's Baby of Shame	Carol Marinelli
The Secret Kept from the Greek	Susan Stephens
A Ring to Secure His Crown	Kim Lawrence
Wedding Night with Her Enemy	Melanie Milburne
Salazar's One-Night Heir	Jennifer Hayward
The Mysterious Italian Houseguest	Scarlet Wilson
Bound to Her Greek Billionaire	Rebecca Winters
Their Baby Surprise	Katrina Cudmore
The Marriage of Inconvenience	Nina Singh

HISTORICAL

Ruined by the Reckless Viscount	Sophia James
Cinderella and the Duke	Janice Preston
A Warriner to Rescue Her	Virginia Heath
Forbidden Night with the Warrior	Michelle Willingham
The Foundling Bride	Helen Dickson

MEDICAL

Mummy, Nurse...Duchess?	Kate Hardy
Falling for the Foster Mum	Karin Baine
The Doctor and the Princess	Scarlet Wilson
Miracle for the Neurosurgeon	Lynne Marshall
English Rose for the Sicilian Doc	Annie Claydon
Engaged to the Doctor Sheikh	Meredith Webber

MILLS_WEB_HB